T0065224

# Oh My God

*Stories for a New World*

BOB MANDEL

ARCHWAY PUBLISHING

Archway Publishing books may be ordered through booksellers or by contacting:

Archway Publishing
1663 Liberty Drive
Bloomington, IN 47403
www.archwaypublishing.com
844-669-3957

ISBN: 978-1-6657-4743-1 (sc)
ISBN: 978-1-6657-4744-8 (e)

Library of Congress Control Number: 2023913695

Print information available on the last page.

Archway Publishing rev. date: 07/28/2023

*I dedicate these stories to Mallie, not a short story, an epic lady, love of my life, an odyssey you continue to create with me.*

# Contents

When the Covid-19 pandemic shut down my business in March, 2020, I bit the bullet like many others and opened up shop on Zoom. I began offering talks once or twice a week to support my clients, students, their friends and families, during the dark days of social distancing and isolation. One day I wrote a simple parable to illustrate a point I wanted to teach. The next day, I wrote another. So it was, I wrote all these stories, one by one, to begin discussions at my Zoom groups. About a year later, a friend suggested I compile the stories into a book. So here you have a parade of parables, prose poems, fables, and conundrums to challenge your mind and open your heart. And, hopefully, some words of wisdom.

Bob Mandel

# Oh My God

Oh my God, the woman at the window said. Oh my God. She was looking at something out of this world. My God, Oh my God, she said over and over again.

She pulled out her iPhone, snapped several pictures, and posted them on all the social media with the caption, OMG. Soon the whole world would know. It would go viral for sure.

Then she went back to look again. She found a magnifying glass so she could observe more closely and there could be no doubt what she was seeing with very own eyes. Yes, what she saw took her breath away. Again. My God, she repeated.

And what she saw was this. On the huge picture window in the living room was a massive spider web at least two meters in diameter. It was picture perfect but too big to be true. Oh my God, she said.

But that wasn't what took her breath away.

On the web she observed the intricate details of little people going up and down and all around, as if attending to their daily activities. God God God, the woman repeated.

And there, at one intersection of two strands in the web, she saw herself, her very own self, though a miniature version. There she was, standing there with a magnifying glass looking at a tiny spider web on a little window. Oh my God.

And even that was not what took her breath away. What it was that made her repeat God's name over and over again was what she beheld at the top of the window, above the web.

Oh my God!

# The Anomalies

And so it came to pass, the world whimpered to an end. It had been a long time coming, so nobody should have been surprised. But still, it came as a shock.

The few survivors were called the Anomalies and they roamed the wasteland searching for what they needed to survive. They were good people and they grew to believe they survived because of their goodness, maybe as people chosen to build a new world.

The Anomalies held meetings to discuss things, such as what to learn from the old world, what not to carry into the new world, and what could be totally different and wonderful. They were nomads, moving mostly on foot, sometimes on old bikes and skateboards. As there was no gasoline, all the old cars lay at the sides of the roads, relics and reminders of an antiquated economy and lost civilization.

One day the Anomalies came to a bridge, a bridge they had never seen. It was a huge golden bridge that went up into the clouds. They had to decide whether to proceed or turn back. Everyone agreed to continue, but when they arrived in the clouds, they were not so sure. So, they divided into three tribes. One would go ahead, another go back. And the third would stay in the clouds.

The result was as such. The one that returned to the old world continued to forage, struggling to adapt and survive. The one that stayed in the clouds stayed in the clouds. And the one that went to the future went to the future, and who knows what happened to them!

# The Prayer

∞∞∞∞∞∞∞∞∞∞∞∞∞

A little girl lit a candle in her tiny bedroom. She prayed. On the other side of the village, a young man heard her prayer. He lit a candle and also prayed. Far away, across the ocean in another land, an old lady in a bed heard the young man, so she sat up, lit a candle, and prayed with him. Almost immediately, an old man in yet a different part of the world, about to light his cigar, changed his mind, lit a candle and clasped his hands. So, it went on, people all over the world hearing the prayer and lighting their candles.

As the days passed and more and more candles glowed, the people who were not praying began to wonder what was happening. Why are all these people praying? What for? Why so many candles burning every night?

Meanwhile, the Candle-lighters, as they came to be called, continued to connect with more and more people, who, hearing the prayer, could not resist lighting new candles. The other people, the Hopeless, as they were named, gradually became more upset, angry, and aggressive, often attacking those in prayer, stealing their candles, and even burning down their homes. But nothing they did could slow down the spread of prayers and candles throughout the world.

Then it came to pass that one day, the sun did not rise, and the Earth entered a period of night without dawn. As the days passed, the Candle-lighters thrived and the Hopeless sunk into an abyss of lost dreams until one day, a little girl, who had just heard the prayer and was about to light her candle, said to her mother. I have an idea. Why don't we invite all the Hopeless into our homes and then we can share our candlelight with them? Her mother smiled, told her father, who told his neighbors, who told their cousins, and so it came to pass that all the Candle-lighters everywhere shared their light and their prayers, their homes and their bread, with all the people living in darkness.

And that is how one little girl in her tiny room, with a prayer and a candle, changed the world.

# The White Hole

<svg width="200" height="20"><text x="0" y="15">◇◇◇◇◇◇◇◇◇◇◇◇◇</text></svg>

A Being of Light came half way across the universe early one morning to see what she could do. She came out of a White Hole which was a reservoir for all the Light in the Universe, a storage facility utilized when certain areas were consumed by excessive darkness.

So it was, a certain Lady of the Light appeared above the Earth and observed the situation below, which was dire. The atmosphere was orange, the ice had melted, causing rising silvery seas that swallowed most all coastal areas, including major cities and tropical islands. Disease was rampant, water scarce, so wars raged for the possession of habitable territories. People were dying faster than they were being born, and all hope was blowing in the wind.

The Lady of Light sighed deeply and mulled over what could be done. After much thought, she came to the following conclusion. She would rewind the complete history of Planet Earth back to the beginning of life, which she would germinate with a very special gene, the Good Gene, nudging the evolution of all life to proceed full steam ahead towards the unconscious but collective desire for universal good.

Moreover, she added a safety valve in the event there was a glitch in the Good Gene. She added a special Epigene, one she called Remember, that would remind people to return to love when they veered off course on their evolutionary journey.

# The No Karma Man

∞∞∞∞∞∞∞∞∞∞∞∞∞∞∞

Once there was a man who achieved the very elevated state of no karma. He had worked very hard on his spiritual development through many lifetimes of karma yoga and arrived at the sacred now with only love and goodness in his heart, no further lessons to be learned. It was quite remarkable, but totally true that this man had become completely pure and self-realized.

And so it came to pass the man died and passed on to the gate of his next lifetime where a certain Guardian of Light greeted him with a huge smile. Congratulations, the Guardian exclaimed to the man. You are the first one who has arrived at this gate with zero karma. I have examined all the akashic records of all your lifetimes and I am perfectly sure that you are a unique soul, perfect in every way.

The man took a deep breath and was left speechless, totally humbled by this revelation of his own perfection. In fact, a single tear of humility formed and fell from his eye, whereupon he smiled and took a tentative step forward, approaching the gate to his reincarnation.

Not so fast, the Guardian said prohibitively. You may not enter. No?, the man said. Have I done something wrong? Some Dharma I failed? No no! Quite the contrary, sir. It is because you have done nothing wrong and everything right, because you are totally self- realized that you have neither possibility nor necessity for any more lifetimes.

"The man, happy but confused, asked. So, my dear Guardian, where is it I go next? Well, smiled the Guardian, shrugging his shoulders. That's just it. You don't go anywhere. You just cease to exist. Poof!"

# The Nowhere Woman

A woman appeared out of nowhere. Nobody knew who she was. One day she arrived and paraded down the street greeting all the townspeople as old friends and distributing gifts to all the children—yoyos, slinkies, and magical pinwheels of colorful fabrics and designs.

Needless to say, she caused quite a stir and nobody knew what to make of her. Was she a witch, an angel-- a benevolent being or a trouble-maker? While the people were engaged in such discussion, the mysterious woman who appeared out of nowhere went about her business, smiling at all passersby and handing out little treasures to the children.

At sunset, she seemed to vanish into thin air. There was not a trace of her and no one had any idea where she lived and spent her nights. Was she homeless, a vagabond, or maybe even a ghost from the spirit world?

Days turned into weeks and months, and a sense of uneasiness descended on the town. Not that the woman had done anything wrong. On the contrary, her kindness continued as before. It was more the lack of explanation for her appearance, let alone behavior, that disturbed a growing number of citizens.

Finally, they held a meeting at the town hall and the next morning a big banner could be seen outside the building, which read, GO BACK TO WHERE YOU BELONG. And so it was, the woman from nowhere disappeared.

However, things did not return to normal, as the town felt a huge pall descend upon it, as if a big hole gripped its heart. All the children wept day and night, and many of their parents felt the same loss. The once happy town became a shadow of its former self.

One day all the children gathered in the park and had a big discussion, which continued for many hours. Finally, they came up with a proposal and that night they put their plan into action. The next morning the banner over town hall had changed. The word GO had been crossed out and replaced, so it now read, COME BACK TO WHERE YOU BELONG.

Thus, it came to be that the following day the woman who appeared out of nowhere returned to the town, happy as a clam, smiling at all passersby, and distributing hula hoops to all the children, who whirled them around their hips as she paraded up and down Main St, home at last.

# God's Shoes

~~~~~~~~~~~~~~~~~~~

Many years ago, there was a man with God in his shoes. Unfortunately, God was sleeping, so the man did not know he was there. He just walked about as though the only thing in his shoes were his own two feet.

It just so happened that this man with a sleeping God in his shoes was a walking man. He loved to walk and walked for miles every day just for the love it, to see who and what he would encounter. He would meet up with all sorts of people, both friends and strangers, and he would tip his hat at each encounter as God continued sleeping in his shoes.

One day he was walking down an empty street out by the railroad tracks when, not looking where he was going, he bumped into an old hobo in the freight yard. He literally bumped into him. The hobo smiled, tipped his hat, and said, beg your pardon, Mister.

Something about the smile that hobo gave him piqued his curiosity and tickled his toes. Is there something I can do for you, asked the man with the sleepy shoes? Whereupon the hobo replied, looking down, well them is mighty fine shoes on your feet and my old raggedy boots are squeezing me something awful, so I was just thinking.... And then he shrugged his shoulders and started to move on.

But the man with God in his shoes made an impulsive decision and they exchanged shoes right there on the spot, whereupon the hobo sauntered off, God waking up and dancing in his shoes, and the first guy felt a buzz in those old raggedy boots. So it was that both men, opposite though they were, walked off from their chance encounter, God awake in their shoes.

# The Magic Mirror

A man goes to a consignment and buys a mirror. He takes it home and hangs it in a hallway. When he looks into the mirror, he sees something odd. Thinking it is a smudge on the mirror, he wipes it clean but he still sees the same thing. This goes on for several days until he decides there is something wrong with the mirror and so he returns it to the consignment shop.

The owner looks into the mirror, smiles, and says it is a perfectly good mirror, exceptional in fact, and he will not give a refund. So, the man drives the mirror over to his girlfriend's house where he leans it against a wall and asks her to look, which she does, then smiles brightly, declaring it a most marvelous mirror. The man shakes his head in disbelief, and they quarrel over the meaning of the mirror, whereupon he takes the mirror and brings it to his office the next morning and strategically places it near the entryway.

The man is a doctor with a large practice so many people, nurses, assistants, and patients pass through daily. As they come and go, stopping to gaze at themselves in the mirror, a broad smile appears on each of their faces, sometimes accompanied by a deep breath and a slight aha. Most amazing of all is that all his patients leave his office feeling a new energy, uplifted and wondrously healed.

And so, it continues, the mirror bringing smiles of joy and wellbeing to all except its owner, who just cannot accept what he sees with his own two eyes, despite corroboration from so many others.

Finally, the good doctor carries his mirror to a friend's house, a psychiatrist, showing him what this mirror does. The friend looks at his reflection, smiles, and laughs giddily. So, he says, you've found yourself a magic mirror, have you? Maybe, his friend says, but it's too weird. What's so weird about seeing an angel hovering above you, the psychiatrist asks? I don't even believe in angels, the man says. Life is not a fairy tale. Quite true, his friend says. Nevertheless, we all need a little magic once in a while, especially these days. There's absolutely nothing wrong with your marvelous mirror. The fault, dear friend, is in your own lack of imagination.

So it is that the man returns home, places the mirror back in his hallway and gazes at it. He sinks to his knees, sighs deeply, tears falling down his face, and he looks up to see a beautiful angel, a magical figure, who smiles at him and reaches out to wipe away his tears.

Bob Mandel

# The Prince of Hope

Out in the hinterlands, in a place called Hope, there lived a young man they called the Prince of Hope. Of course, he was not really a prince by title, but he had a princely demeanor, a kind of grace and grandeur that caused people to look twice.

Not that he was arrogant or trying to call attention to himself. In fact, quite the opposite, he was shy, quiet, and quite embarrassed when he heard folks whispering, there goes the prince. They said the prince had a smile that could light up a room, bring cheer to the cheerless, and heal the lame. Perhaps it was because the prince himself had a certain disability, which he hid quite well but which awakened great empathy in him.

So it was that when the Great War came and all the young men went off to fight overseas, the Prince of Hope was left behind. People began to wonder what was wrong with the lad, then they began to talk, and pretty soon the prince was no longer referred to as a prince but, rather, as a draft-dodger, traitor, or unpatriotic bum. Meanwhile, the prince quietly volunteered his services at Hope General Hospital, continuing to light up the lives of the patients with his kind-hearted smiles and gentle hands.

In time, wounded soldiers occupied a good number of the beds, and the prince spent many a day sitting by their sides, whispering words of comfort and hope. It came to pass that one day a nurse appeared and their eyes locked, and they began to walk down Kind Blessing Boulevard, hand in hand. They didn't talk very much but it was clear they had taken a liking to each other and then one day she asked him what was wrong with him.

So, they sat on a park bench and he told her about the clubfoot he was born with, how it kept him apart from the other children, prevented him from fighting for his country, and caused him so much shame and suffering. She looked at him and placed a hand on his face, saying gently. That's not what's wrong with you. That's your gift. That's what makes you the Prince of Hope.

# The Listener

A wonderful lady from the boondocks was a very good listener. In fact, all she did was listen, every hour of every waking day. Nobody knew her name so they called her the Listener.

She listened to children who told her all their problems and the problems of their parents. She listened to parents who told her all their worries about their children and their fears for the future. She listened to the beggars who asked why they had to suffer so much. She listened to the men of good fortune who asked why there were so many beggars. She listened to the sick, the lame, the blind, and the deaf, all of whom asked, why me? As the Listener never spoke, she could not answer their questions. She only listened, nodded her head in understanding, occasionally sighing or gently placing a hand on a shoulder, patting a back, or lifting the chin of a child.

But when she went home each night, her daily listening done, she kneeled by her altar and prayed for each and everyone whose story she heard, whether a scruffy street urchin, a hopeless invalid, or an ungrateful man of good fortune.

So it came to pass that the Listener grew old, her body weary, and her ears tired of so much listening. Yet her eyes kept on twinkling, especially when she saw the hope in the little children's eyes.

Finally, she became bed-ridden and knew the end was near. She closed her eyes and breathed, listening to the sound of air. And as the Listener began to let go of her life, she heard from above the voices of angels calling to her. Grace, they said. Grace. We are listening to you.

# The Phantom Hand

The man grips his wife's hand and feels its warm, familiar fingers curl around his, the soft pillow underneath.

He remembers the first time he held that hand.

They are walking side by side on a sand dune up on the Cape, alone one chilly Autumn day. She stumbles and falls, twisting her ankle. He reaches for her, giving his hand and taking hers. The electricity is palpable. They walk back to the car hand in hand, she limping, their connection firm and knowing.

He feels the wedding ring and twirls it around, a tear hanging precariously at the edge of his eye, a tear containing the memory of when everything changed, the visit to the neurologist, the scan, the cognitive test, and the diagnosis.

That was when her hand began to disappear, but the feeling inside it stayed, retaining a certain warmth which could always warm the coldness in his lonely limbs. Whenever he walks the dog on a cold winter morning, he slides back to bed, placing his hand in hers, and she whispers, so cold. He replies, so warm.

Lying on his side, he moves a single finger in a circle on the palm of the hand, observing the lines he cannot read. He remembers when they consulted a palm reader, who told them they would be together forever because forever was etched in both their palms.

Massaging her knuckles, he senses all the hard work they have endured, all the seeds they have planted and weeds they have pulled from the garden-- her spectacular dahlias, zinnias, peonies, plus the blueberry bushes, grape tomatoes, cucumbers, zucchinis and eggplants. Moving down to her wrist, he feels where the carpal tunnel shut down, taking away the feeling in her fingers, numbing her touch, gnarling those beautiful fingers.

Eventually, the man falls into a long sleep, her hand in his, notwithstanding all the loss, lingering, and longing. One morning, after many sleepless nights, he finally wakes up and finds himself holding the most beautiful hand in the world. It shines like a brilliant sunrise. It seems to smile at him as if saying, a new day has dawned. He holds the hand tight, wanting to absorb perfect love, but the fingers wiggle, whispering. Please, let go.

# The Turned Around Woman

There once was a woman whose head was turned around backwards. Everyone thought she had escaped from some freak show down at the carnival. It was very awkward because she had to walk backwards so she could see ahead. People always gave her second looks when they encountered her even though she was well known all over the borough. You just couldn't help it.

She hadn't always been that way. Back in the day, she walked down the street looking straight ahead until one day it all changed. That was the day she felt someone following her. So, she began looking behind her all the time, suspicious, afraid, and her mind all twisted. She never actually saw anyone following her, but she was convinced he was there, whether a spook, a stranger, or just a professional follower. Anyway, so it came to pass that the woman's head became turned around backwards.

One day the woman was walking backwards down a country road, carrying a bag of groceries. A head of her she saw a man approaching. Strangely, he was also walking backwards, facing her. He came up to her, face- to-face backwards. What happened to you, he asked? She told him her story. Then she asked him for his.

Well, it was like this, he said. I was following this girl I had taken a liking to, but she kept turning her head to see who was following her. So I kept turning my own because I didn't want her to see me. Finally, one day I couldn't turn it back.

I see, the woman said. They both laughed and then the man said. Well, I guess one good turn deserves another. And with that, he took her bag of groceries, turned around, and they both walked off together.

# The Wounded Man

◇◇◇◇◇◇◇◇◇◇◇◇◇

A young man lay wounded by the side of a road by a pile of dead leaves. Another man came along, kicked him twice, and continued on his way. A woman came next and, seeing the wounded young man, shook her head, crossed the road and continued on her way. Then came a man in white robes. He bent over, touched the young man, and said, I will pray for you, then promptly forgot about him.

Finally, a farmer came, put the wounded young man in the back of his cart, and took him home. He and his wife took care of the man for several days, bathing, feeding, and treating his wounds, all the time in silence.

One morning, the young man came down for breakfast and the farmer said, tell us what happened to you. The young man said nothing until breakfast was done, after which he told his story. As I am a Jew, I was attacked. As I am a black man, I was beaten. As I am a refugee I was tortured. So it was I lay on the side of the road, ignored by all until you came along.

The farmer shook his head in disbelief and then asked. But who are you? Really, who? The young man looked in his eyes and replied, I am simply a child of the universe trying to make the world a better place. And who are you? Really, who? The farmer smiled, reached out his hand, and said, I am like you.

Bob Mandel

# The Barista

A barista from the sunny side of the street is very happy. As he serves each customer, he adds, Have a REALLY great day, plus an infectious grin. Everyone feels uplifted by his spirit. And the coffee is dynamite.

One day a masked man enters and pulls a gun, demanding the barista hand over all the cash, which he does, plus what's in his pockets. Have a REALLY great day, he says to the thief with that infectious grin. I am having just that, the masked man replies and turns to leave. Would you like a cup of mighty fine coffee before you head out? The thief scratches his head, says. I can't think why not.

So it comes to pass that he slips off his mask and the two men sit down with their cups of Joe, the thief savoring the mighty brew, and commenting. Well, this is a mighty fine brew. What is your secret ingredient? The barista smiles and says, lean over and I'll whisper it in your ear. So he does, his ear savoring the secret after which he cracks up in knee-slapping laughter.

When he quiets down and is getting ready to leave, he says, I just can't walk out of here with all your money, I mean, it just wouldn't be right after all you've done for me. And so it is he returns the cash.

The barista looks at the man, smiles, and says. That is most generous of you, kind sir. You have a REALLY great day. The man replies, I reckon I'll do just that, then, patting the man with the infectious grin on the back, he departs.

# The Fountain of Hope

〰〰〰〰〰〰〰〰〰

There once existed a Fountain of Hope in the old part of town. It was a beautiful marble fountain shaped like a clam with three golden angels overhead. The fountain was said to answer all who voiced hope.

Needless to say, people came from all over, expressing hope for their hopeless family and friends, whether sick relatives, troubled children, bankrupt businesses, or homeless people wandering the streets. It was quite a sight, such an outpouring of love and compassion, and many tears filled the fountain along with the angel water.

Although it appeared that hope was fulfilled for many of these supplicants as more and more flooded the fountain, more likely it was the same ones kept returning with the same unfulfilled hope. Sometimes it was so crowded, you couldn't get close enough to the angels to ask for your hope at all.

It came to pass that one day a distinguished looking elderly man approached the Fountain of Hope, politely maneuvering his way through the mob until he managed to get quite near the angels. He removed his fedora and gazed up at the angels. Taking a deep breath, he was about to express his hope, but he lost it. He could not remember what he came to hope for.

So, he went home and tried to remember and returned the following day, with the same result. He repeated the same ritual every day for a week, but he never could remember his hope.

Finally, one day he summoned all his courage, went back to the Fountain of Hope, fell to his knees, and prayed. Dear Fountain, please remind me what it is I most hope for. That night, he had a lucid dream in which he received the response to his request from the fountain.

He woke up before dawn with a broad grin spread across his face, hurried back down to the Fountain of Hope, where he expressed the hope he now remembered. My hope, dear Fountain and beloved angels, my sincerest hope is that everyone else's hope comes to pass.

# *Leaving Home*

There exists a bridge they call the Bridge of Light, the Magnificent Bridge of Light. Not everyone is permitted to cross. You have to be a special kind of person and meet certain requirements.

So it is that one day a lovely, young woman arrives at the Bridge of Light, ready for her journey. She turns to wave good-bye to her mother, father, and two little brothers. They are all crying. It is so hard to leave them. So, she runs back to them and says she will not go, she will wait one more year. Her father says, thank God you've come to your senses. Let's go home. But her mom, the firm one, says, no, you must go now. This is your time.

So, suitcase in hand, she ventures forth back onto the Bridge of Light. The bridge is beautiful, glowing, full of hope and faith, peace and love. She takes a breath, but then she breaks down in tears, missing her family so very much. Then she remembers something she forgot. So, she runs back to her family, who are still standing there, waving good-bye. I forgot my candles, she says. Her father replies at once, I hid them to test you. If you can't remember your candles, how can you possibly survive on a Bridge of Light. Leave her alone, her mother says. You need to let go of each other.

So, the young lady embarks yet again on her adventure on the magical bridge. This time, she proceeds further, learning respect and forgiveness, and how to affirm herself and others. She comes to an island, a resting point, where she lights a candle and gives thanks for her family and newfound independence. Then, in a flash, she is sobbing like a newborn baby, missing her father and little brothers so much. Her mother, a little less. She whips out her iPhone and texts her dad that she cannot go on, she is not prepared, she needs a good night kiss and a cup of hot chocolate. Her dad replies immediately. Come home. But her mom sends an instant follow-up message. Don't you dare.

So, the young woman reluctantly embraces her independence or banishment, whichever it is, and the next morning she forages towards her next adventure, perhaps a young man to sweep her off her feet or, even better, a romance that will place her feet firmly on the ground, the ground being the Bridge of Light.

She stops and lights another candle, full of hope. She takes a breath and, feeling complete with the family of her birth, she feels ready for her new life. As she looks across the bridge, there he is waiting for her, Prince Charming or Prince Alarming, God knows.

# The Man God Needed

∞∞∞∞∞∞∞∞∞∞∞∞∞

A man who has led an ideal life arrives in Heaven. God asks, what are you doing here? The man says, well, I've lived a good life—a good son, brother, husband, father and grandfather, a successful businessman, generous, kind, a contributor to the community, pacifist and advocate for human rights around the world. I reckoned I deserve to put a foot in Heaven.

God replies, absolutely, I welcome your foot, but not the rest of you. While I cannot argue with anything you have said in your favor and totally agree with your judgment of why your foot has earned the right to be here in Heaven—while your life has been golden, without blemish and fully worthy, it is because of all your extraordinary qualities that I still need you to do my work on Earth. I need saints like you to stay alive, not die off. You are precious to me. So, get back down there and get those children of mine, your brothers and sisters, to see the light, both in themselves and in each other, and behave accordingly. I will reserve you a space up here for when your job is done.

# The Elephant Boy

A baby is crying in a field way out near the Bay of Sweet Dreams. A kind cow comes along and gives him some milk. The next day the baby is crying again so a friendly fox brings him a blanket. The third day when the baby cries a loving elephant approaches and, curling him in her trunk, carries him away.

Thus, the baby is raised in a herd of elephants and grows up believing he is an elephant. One day a man comes along and takes the baby who is now a young boy and, thinking he is an elephant, ties him by his ankle to a tree so he won't run off. The man does this every day and the boy comes to believe he is an elephant tied to a tree. When the boy grows into an adolescent, the man no longer ties him to a tree, knowing elephants learn to believe they are always tied to a tree and thus never run off. So, the boy who is now an adolescent believes this whole story and does not go anywhere.

Later, a beautiful young woman comes along and, seeing the now handsome young man, smiles at him. The man does not understand why a beautiful woman would smile at an elephant like that. He tells her. She looks at him, smiles again, and says. I thought an elephant never forgets. Don't you remember me, the kind cow who bought you milk when you were a baby crying in the field.

Bob Mandel

# The Calico Cat

✕✕✕✕✕✕✕✕✕✕✕✕✕✕✕✕

There once was a woman who wanted to rise up. She had been pushed down all her life, first by her father whom she loved and obeyed, then by her husband who ruled the roost, and finally by her three daughters, whom she could not control.

So, she ended up in the middle of her life, divorced, alone, and wanting to rise up. In truth, she knew she was a lost soul and needed to find herself. First, she sought wise counseling. She went to a psychologist who offered her psychoanalysis. Then she asked a life coach who suggested motivational therapy. She joined a group of women who loved to complain about men.

Finally, she visited a shaman who said she needed a soul journey. She signed up for the soul journey and this is where it took her.

Rio. While sitting in a café in Rio de Janeiro, enjoying a double espresso, a gorgeous calico cat jumped onto her lap and brushed his tail across her face. Then he told her this. You have zero self-esteem, absolutely zero. Maybe sub-zero. If you don't love yourself as much as I love myself, you will never rise up. With that, he leapt up and vanished into thin air.

She knew the cat had nailed her, but when she returned from her journey and the shaman asked her what she had discovered, she replied. I need a cat. So, the shaman brought her a cat and it was the same calico cat from her soul journey, and that calico cat smiled at her and said, you're not going to escape yourself that easily.

# A Man with No Opinion

There lived a man with no opinion. When asked about the weather, he would say, can't complain. Whether the weather changed, his opinion remained the same. It was the same with everything. His wife asked him what he wanted for dinner. I don't care, he replied. When his son asked about a career, whether to be a doctor, lawyer or bee keeper, he had no preference.

Thus it was, the man with no opinion drifted through his life until one day he became a new man. He was walking down the Boulevard of Hope when he noticed the children were dressed up in costumes. It was Halloween. Something moved inside him. Then he remembered there was a full moon that night, a super moon, and the thing moved a little more. Finally, he recalled it was a blue moon and the moving thing kicked him in the gut.

So it was, when the sun went down and the moon came up the man with no opinion found himself walking down by the river, then across the old bridge, and finally slowly but steadily up to the pinnacle of the hill from which he could see the river valley below, bathed in the glow of super moonlight.

Upon reaching the summit, the man stripped off all his clothes and stood stark naked upon the cliff, where he raised his arms high towards the sky, his fists clenched in tight balls. And then he began to howl. From that place deep down in his gut where the something had moved, he howled. And he howled and he howled and he howled like the wildest wolf in all the land. And so it was that the man with no opinion voiced his very loud opinion.

Bob Mandel

# The Worrisome Woman

◇◇◇◇◇◇◇◇◇◇◇◇◇◇◇◇

There lived a woman who could not stop worrying. She worried over everything and everyone.

It began when she was a young girl and she worried her parents would die. Then they did. So, she worried about her baby brother, who also died. She ended up worrying about the whole doggone world, as well as worrying about her worries causing the things she worried about to occur. When she passed a friend in the street, she would say, I'm worried about you. Her friend would say, please don't worry about me.

So, she would shift what she called her worryscope to observe another target, be it the bank teller, the gas station attendant, or the local florist, all of who would raise their hands and proclaim. No worries, my friend.

So it was that one day she walked down on the beach, worrying she might not have any more use for her worryscope when she noticed a big old walrus, who was sobbing uncontrollably, drowning in his own tears. She approached him, sighed, and said, I suppose you too are going to tell me not to worry about you. No, he sniffled, not at all. Please, please worry about me. All my life, nobody worried about me. They told me never to worry about a thing, and so I didn't, not even when I realized I didn't know how to swim. The result of it all is here I am, all washed up, wasting away, my last breath approaching with each passing wave.

So, the woman who loved to worry said, not to worry, poor walrus, I will worry about you all the days of my life. And so, she walked off smiling, leaving one happy worrisome walrus in her wake.

# The Shadow

Once there was a shadow in search of the light. He knew it had to be somewhere as a shadow can only be seen in the light. But somehow, he was a shadow lost in the dark.

He looked all over, in the mountains, valleys, seas and of course the sky, but the light seemed to be hiding. So he went to see the Shadow Shaman who told him to do a journey to retrieve the light of his soul. He did it.

He found himself in a cave standing opposite his light shadow, a fire burning between them. His brother said to him, so you want me back now. Yes, the shadow replied, I miss your light. You should not have sent me away. The shadow felt tears well in his eyes. You're right, he sobbed, I envied you your light. I hated you. I blocked you completely out of my mind.

The light shadow came around the fire and put an arm around his brother. Brother, I love you. You can block me out of your mind but you can never separate yourself from me. I am a part of you. What's mine is yours. The dark shadow looked up and said, I recognize the truth in your words. Please forgive me. The light shadow kissed his brother and replied, because you are innocent, there is nothing to forgive. And so it was that the shadow returned to the light.

Bob Mandel

# The Girl Who Levitated

<svg>◇◇◇◇◇◇◇◇◇◇◇◇◇◇◇</svg>

A young girl is walking home from school when she notices she is levitating. There she is, six feet clear off the ground. At first, she is amazed, but, floating even higher, she becomes lightheaded and unable to find her center of gravity. Finally, when she reaches a cloud, a huge blast of wind grabs her, tumbling her to the ground where she bangs her head. When she sits up, she doesn't remember a thing.

She goes home, sits down for milk and cookies, her mother asks, how was your day? And she replies, same old same old. That night she dreams she is levitating the same as in real life, floating up as before, the wind blowing her down and banging her head. When she awakens, she doesn't remember the dream.

Later, she walks home on the same road, again levitating and drifting up to the clouds where she meets a wizard who tells her she must remember her supernatural experiences and she should tell her mother about them. He gives her a magic pill which he says will help her have lucid memory. Then a big wind blows her down, she bangs her head, and when she opens her eyes, she cannot recall a thing.

So she goes home, sits down for milk and cookies, and when her mom asks how was your day? She replies, same old, same old. Then her mom notices a little pill on the table and tells her to take her vitamin, which she does, and then suddenly she remembers everything. She tells her mother as the wizard instructed and when she's done, her mom scratches her head and, forgetting everything her daughter has said, repeats. So, same old, same old.

# The Disappointed Man

A long time ago there lived a disappointed man. He was disappointed in anything and everything, anyone and everyone. His wife, who once had seemed such a promising prospect, had turned out to be a sourpuss. His two kids took after their mom. They all belonged to the Committee of Complainers.

His work as a fisherman out at the Bay of Sweet Dreams took a toll on his health, chronic pain gripping his back. His house, which he had built with his own hands, was a money pit, always needing attention and repair. Thus, the man was living a life of perpetual disappointment. On a treadmill of despair, a list of complaints as long as the Mississippi River.

One day he was having a disappointing whiskey at the local watering hole when the guy sitting on the stool next to him turned and said, Aint life grand? The disappointed man looked up in disbelief, and replied, You've got to be kidding. And then he volleyed off a litany of complaints about everything that was rotten this side of the state of Denmark, so to speak. When he had completed his whining, the guy sitting next to him stood up and said, follow me.

So, they went outside, got on the guy's Harley, and drove off to the sea. When they were standing on the Great Cliffs of Doubt, as they were called, looking out at the endless sea, the guy said to the disappointed man. Look at all that damn beauty, Mister! Would you rather praise the Lord or jump off this cliff? So, the disappointed man scratched his chin and replied, I reckon I'd go for the second option, whereupon the other guy pushed him off the cliff down to the sea below.

When the disappointed man emerged from the frigid water, he took a breath and, realizing he was still alive, shouted up to the guy up on the cliff, Praise the Lord!

Bob Mandel

# The Pushy Woman

~~~~~~~~~~~~~~~~~~~~

There once was a pushy woman from the hill country. She pushed everyone. For her, pushing was a way of life, a religion. For example, she pushed her two children, first when they were born and then when they were growing up. She pushed them to be the best they could be, at home, in school, everywhere. She pushed her husband to improve as a man and a businessman because she loved him and wanted him to be all he could be. Plus, she wanted more money. Most of all, she pushed herself because she never felt satisfied, no matter how much she did each day, no matter how much she pushed others. She always felt something was missing and so she pushed herself more.

Then one day everything changed. The pushy woman from the hill country was driving her car, an old beat-up VW minibus over a really big hill in order to visit her parents in the Highlands who were in need of some serious pushing. On the way to their house, her car broke down. So, she got out and began to push the car up the mountain.

It was rough going until a stranger came along and began to push her while she pushed the car. Then another stranger came along and began pushing the first stranger. In a short time there was a long line of good people pushing each other as they pushed the pushy woman who pushed her car clear up over the mountain and down to her parents' house.

When she arrived, her parents said, so, what will you be pushing us about today? The pushy woman, said, well I guess nothing. I'm just about all pushed out.

# The Healer in High Demand

There once was a healer in high demand. She lived out in the boondocks, but could often be found throughout the land, administering her substantial gifts.

One unrelenting Winter it seemed everyone needed her healing. The young ones had their seasonal sickness, the old ones had their elderly illness, the middle ones were breaking their bones every which way, and the pregnant ones all seemed to be having their babies at the same time. No rest for this healer. At night she would dream about countless needy hands reaching out to touch her, waking up in a deep sweat, despite the frigid wind howling and rattling her windows.

As the season dragged on, the healer, her heart heavy, grew so weary of the laying on of hands that her feet would no longer carry her from town to town or door to door. So it was that one night she plopped down on her bed and the next morning she couldn't get up. She was plum stuck to the mattress, all worn out and in need of some serious healing herself.

Days passed and the healer stayed glued to her sheets. The people who needed her healing hands grew restless. Eventually, they climbed out of their own beds and trekked one by one across the frigid land, lined up outside her door in demand of her healing hands. They knocked on the door, called out for her to open up, and when she didn't, they busted down that door and descended upon her bedroom where they found her still cemented to her bed.

What do you all want, she asked them? When they all called out in one huge cacophony the names of their ailments-- leg, head, stomach, heart, liver, and so forth, she threw her hands in the air and shushed them. Listen up, all you crybabies. I reckon if you're well enough to charge across the hill on a wretched day like this, my healing has done a good enough job without my going nowhere.

Bob Mandel

# The Onion Man

◇◇◇◇◇◇◇◇◇◇◇◇◇◇◇◇

In a remote land when time was just dawning, a man who woke up one morning and thought he was an onion. It was a preposterous thought because in his logical mind he knew he was a man, a farmer, a husband, and a father. But he awakened to feel for certain he had become an onion.

So, without discussing his situation, he went out into the field to talk to the other onions. They looked at him and, without any disagreement, they all nodded their heads, recognizing him as one of their own and welcoming him into the fraternity of onion-hood.

And so he asked them, what do I have to learn to be a good onion? There was a great murmur across the field of onions as they discussed how best to advise their new member. You have to peel away at it, one finally said. Yes, don't be in a rush. One layer at a time. They all joined in with their opinions. To be a good onion is to be a good contributor to the community of onions. You must integrate all your individual skins. Be translucent. Be sweet. Don't make too many other onions cry. So it was that the new onion absorbed all the wisdom of the older and more experienced onions.

When he completed his apprenticeship, he returned to his family and tried to apply his knowledge to his human life. The result was a disaster. His daughter said she didn't know him anymore; he had become a vegetable. His wife broke down in tears, saying he lost his spine, he was like soup. Just be yourself, for God's sake, his eldest son snapped. We liked you that way.

Oy, the Onion Man thought as he made his way back out to the Field of Onions. After recounting his reception upon returning home, the fraternity of Onions all hummed and nodded in understanding. There is one thing we forgot to tell you, one said. Yes, perhaps the most important thing, said another. A good Onion, a really good Onion, spreads himself throughout all his skins. Yes, said another one behind him, to be a genuine

Onion is to blend in rather than stand out. And, said a third one in the back row, that could pose problems in your field of humankind. I mean, with your need for individual attention. Imagine, concluded a little feller up front, if your type discovered there was nothing special about being an individual.

# The Thank You Man

<><><><><><><><><><><><>

There lived a young man who said thank you all the time. Wherever he went, whomever he encountered, he immediately said thank you, as though each person's name was Thank You. He would say thank you to the grocer for his avocados and tomatoes, thank you to the bank teller when he deposited his money, and even thank you to the trees as he walked through the woods. Thank you to the sky and thank you to the river, thank you to the thistles and thank you to the crab grass. He was indiscriminating about his thank yous and thus you would think he was the most grateful man in the world.

So it came to pass that one day, Thanksgiving by chance, he was sitting around a table with family and friends, of course giving profuse thanks to each and every person when suddenly his brother raised a hand and said, stop. You know, my brother, while I am sure we all deeply appreciate your expression of gratitude, you should consider the thanks all of us wish to give you. Consider also, everything you thank us for is our pleasure to give to you and no thanks are called for. It is our honor. There was a big hush at the table and the young man dropped his head, sighed, and simply said, sorry.

For some days after, he walked around saying sorry, sorry, sorry to everyone and everything. Then he stopped talking forever. He just walked around in somber silence.

Later, they found his body floating down the river, the sky above him and the trees by his side. People came from all over to see. A young boy pointed and shouted, Look, it's the Thank You Man.

# The Batty Old Angel

Have you heard the one about the batty old angel? She was a sight to behold, eyes popping out of their sockets, hair tangled down to her waist, and dressed in rags and rejects from consignment shops. You can only imagine.

Nevertheless, the old hag didn't have a mean bone in her body and would offer a helping hand to anyone in need, though if truth be told, who would ask? Thus she was a very kind and lonely batty old woman, her goodness all rolled up in a ball inside herself.

She lived on the fifth floor of a six-story tenement building, which she huffed and puffed her way up every day. Her neighbors consisted of young newlyweds, a few families with toddlers, and one very old man in a wheelchair who never ventured out. How could he? He lived in the attic of a six-floor walk up. All these neighbors ignored her, considering her a batty old woman, although in their hearts they recognized she was a kind soul.

It came to pass that one night lightning struck, in the middle of an August heatwave, and the brownstone went up in flames, the firemen came, and the Batty Old Woman showed her true colors. At the time, she was preparing a very fine watermelon gazpacho, a perfect soup for a sultry Summer evening. She could hear all her neighbors running for dear life, carrying babies and children in their arms.

Savoring one last taste of soup, the Batty Old Woman remembered the man in the wheelchair above her, and, eyes rolling, climbed up the stairs, opened his door, and began her rescue of him. Unfortunately, she tripped, twisting and falling ungracefully forward, extending her arms which miraculously grew like railroad tracks down all six flights, so the gentleman on wheels rolled down the stairs upon her outstretched body without a hitch. In the end she didn't make it, but the man in the wheelchair survived.

So it was, she became quite a legend throughout the land, and a statue was erected depicting the Batty Old Angel laying down her life for the Wheelchair Man.

# Mountain Climber

In the old days, the New World was dotted with hills and mountains before it settled down into flatlands. Back then, a man found himself climbing a mountain. Where he lost himself is anybody's guess.

But there he was, searching. He climbed and he climbed and the going grew harder and steeper, but he made steady progress and at first the pinnacle seemed to be getting closer. At a certain point he paused and found some shade to get out of the sun. He drank some water and wondered how he would feel when he reached the top. Then he resumed walking.

As he climbed further, he suddenly had the sensation that the peak was not getting closer at all and he was not making any real progress, and, in fact, he felt like he was just walking in place. This realization caused him to break out in a sweat and a panic attack. He considered the possibility that he might be getting delirious and perhaps should turn back, but just as he was trying to decide a storm picked up so he pitched his tent and hunkered down for the night.

When he woke up, he felt reinvigorated so he continued his climb. At a certain moment, he noticed a man coming down, approaching him. When the man was in front of him, they both stopped and stared at each other. He was looking at himself. There's no need to go to the top, the man said, laughing. The only thing to do once you get there is come back down. So, the two men walked back own together. Thus, it was that the climbing man found himself.

# The Beggar

◇◇◇◇◇◇◇◇◇◇◇◇◇

A man searches for God. He wants to talk to Him. He looks in nature, in the gardens, forests, rivers, and seas. He sees much beauty, but he does not find God. He climbs the highest mountains, above the clouds, and he is impressed but unconvinced of God's presence.

He visits museums and concert halls, viewing the most beautiful paintings and listening to breathtaking music, but God remains elusive.

Finally, one day he is walking down the street and a beggar comes up to him. I hear you're looking for me, the beggar says. You? The man is confused. Who are you, he asks? I'm the One you're looking for, the beggar replies. The man stares at the beggar, incredulous.

You are God, he asks? The one and only, replies the beggar. But you look like a beggar, the man states. I am a beggar, the beggar replies. What are you begging for? You're God Almighty. The beggar takes a deep breath and says. Right now I'm begging to know why you were looking for me. I wanted to talk to you, the man says. You are talking to me, the beggar replies. I guess I am. Do you need anything, the man asks the beggar? Right now, I need to go around the corner because there's another guy looking for me. See you later. And the beggar walks off.

Bob Mandel

# The Psychiatrist

◇◇◇◇◇◇◇◇◇◇◇◇◇◇◇◇

There once was a psychiatrist who needed help. He lived out by the cliffs when a huge hurricane hit, flooding his house and knocking out the power. This was in the day before cell phones, computers, and even Elvis. The psychiatrist found himself stranded on his roof in torrential downpours, considering his situation.

The water was rapidly rising, there was not another person in sight, and he neither knew how to swim nor owned a boat. So, you can see why I say he needed help. His options were few, or none. He could sit on his roof and wait for the end to come. Be stoic. Secondly, he could wait for the end to come and pray it would not come. As he was an atheist, prayer seemed a little disingenuous, especially at such a late date.

As the rain continued to pour down on him, a third option suddenly popped into his waterlogged mind. He could analyze himself and figure out how and why he had come to such a dire predicament. At the very least, a good self-analysis would keep him occupied until, well, you know what.

So, first he thinks, I was born at the wrong time, during the pogrom in Russia, a huge burden to my parents, who were over their heads in love and in debt at the time. My mother confessed to me, she wished I had never been born. In fact, she took numerous potions and herbs to try to abort me. Then, on the other side of the ocean, I married the wrong woman who was over her head in love with another man while I was still thinking about what my mother had said. Finally, I got divorced, three cheers for that, and I bought this dream house by the sea, which I enjoyed for exactly one year to the day when the stock market crashed in 1929. And now, three years later, I'm over my head in debt and about to be the same in water!

The psychiatrist continues to analyze himself, the water now rising onto the roof. Finally, as he is flailing in the crashing waters, fighting for his life, he realizes the real reason he is in such dire need of help.

As his whole life flashes by him like a movie in reverse, he stands up on the roof and, waving two fists against the raging storm, and cries out, Help! Please, God, help me. Then he falls to his knees, sobbing and embracing himself. He hears a whirling sound, looks up, and a helicopter is hovering. A rope is tossed down towards him. He reaches up, then suddenly remembering he is afraid of heights, cries out. Oh my God.

# The Last Question



A day came when God announced He was creating the University of Heaven. When the people asked why, he explained. In the past it was possible for people to leap directly from Earth to Heaven, after having lived a good life, but now the leap is more complicated and we need a university to ease the transition. The people nodded their heads in agreement and went home.

When the university opened, everyone wanted admission, but standards were high. You had to be a good person, kind, compassionate, generous—near perfect. Moreover, you had to have references to prove your worthiness. So, in fact, very few people made it.

After four years of grueling studies, lab work, and community service, a handful of students remained. God called them all into His office and said, I address you as the first graduating class of the University of Heaven. I am immensely proud of you and would very happily send you off to Heaven to fulfill your destiny to bless all beings everywhere. However, there is one more little question I ask you to answer in order to proceed on your journey. The question is this. What are you looking to find in Heaven?

Each of the first four students thought about his answer and then answered like this. Love. Peace. Harmony. Happiness. There was only one student who remained silent. Finally, she said to God, I'm sorry, my Lord, but I am still looking for the answer. So, God said to the first four to stay on Earth and find love, peace, harmony, and happiness. To the girl he said, go forth with my blessings, young lady, and when you find the answer, please let me be the first to know.

# The Pall

One day a pall fell over a city, nobody knew why. One day the sky was blue, the next morning, poof, a terrible pall!

At first, people ignored it, going about their business as if nothing had changed, but as the days turned into weeks, the heaviness grew. The community leaders gathered to make a plan as they always did. They came up with all sorts of wild suggestions such as constructing a huge windmill to blow the pall away, creating a gigantic mirror to reflect the light of the sun and burn it off, or building a great ladder to climb above the pall and drown it with buckets of water. In the end, the meeting disbanded with no plan of action.

The pall grew heavier on the people's minds.

On a certain Sunday a stranger arrived downtown and, seeing the pall above, walked about, taking measurements. When he was done, he told the people that the problem was not the pall but the buildings. They were facing the wrong way and had to be turned around. For some reason, they all believed the stranger and set about gathering cranes, lifting, and turning each building around, one by one until the whole darn city was facing the opposite way. Then they waited, but nothing happened.

The people grew restless, thinking the stranger was a snake oil salesman. The stranger, scratched his beard, looked around, then noticed something and exclaimed aha, upon which he marched over to a little dog house, turned it around, and presto pronto, the pall lifted as if a giant sheet was removed from the heavens above, and the sun returned.

The next day, the stranger left and the pall returned, so a boy turned the dog house around again and it went away.

Bob Mandel

# The Really Big Man

‹◇◇◇◇◇◇◇◇◇◇◇◇◇◇◇◇◇›

Something big was coming down the cobblestone hill, you could feel it rumbling. So, when Michael, an old guy who wasn't all there, strolled down by the old park, little did he know what to make of it when he met up with a man called Mo, a man he both remembered yet didn't quite recognize. Mo was something big alright, a mighty man in stature and goodness, one hunk of a beautiful man.

Howdy, Mo, Michael said, scratching his head, remember me? Mo nodded and smiled a big radiant grin, and said, sure do. Never forget you. Without you, I wouldn't be the man I am today. And then Mo laughed out loud and continued on his way. Michael stood there, moved by Mo's words, but somewhat dumbfounded.

Later, Michael was sitting at the counter at the ice cream parlor, nursing his afternoon cup of Joe when a little feller sat down beside him and ordered a hot fudge Sunday. They sat like that for a while before the little feller said to Michael, you remember me? Michael scratched his head and said, can't say that I do. Care to refresh my memory?

Well, you see, Mr. Mike, I am little Mo, you know, the Mo before he was so big and amazing. Maybe you don't remember but one day back when he was me, you found me all bruised and beaten, covered in blood, mud and tears down by the lake. You picked me up and said, Little Feller, some day you gonna be a great big feller. And when you get to be the biggest of all men, big enough to push all the others around, you know what, you won't do it. You know why? Here's why. You're gonna be a really big man, that's why. So, Mr. Mike, without you, I wouldn't be the big man I am now.

# The Kind Wife

A woman from a faraway land is overflowing with kindness. She showers everyone she encounters with buckets of kindness. On the train to work, her smile is so infectious everyone in her car begins to laugh and sing. In her office, while she is at a meeting, she spontaneously tells all her co-workers how wonderful they are, how grateful she is to know them, and what a great blessing they are to her. On her way home, she buys chocolate for her children and a bottle of fine wine for her husband, and when she enters her home, she radiates love and goodness, and her joy and enthusiasm cause her whole family to rejoice.

Later, in bed with her husband, he turns to her and says this. I just don't know how you do it. How can you secrete such amazing love and kindness in the midst of everything that's going on? She blinks her eyes several times and asks him what he means, what's going on, is there something she's missing. So, he tells her that the world is in dire straits, plague is rampant, the climate is going down the toilet, people have lost all respect and the leaders of the world have neither manners, scruples, empathy, or decency. Women are abused, people of color are beaten, and children are dying of thirst, hunger, and disease everywhere. It is so sad, my love, his voice shaking.

His wife looks at him with a tear in her eye. My poor, dear darling, your great big heart overwhelms me. I am so blessed by your love, understanding, and compassion. You are surely the kindest man in the whole wide world.

# The Eyes of Beauty

A young boy had a gift that for him was not a gift. You see, this boy could see the future. He said his eyes were ugly because they saw so many ugly things He saw people getting sick, old people uncared for, and babies with no mothers. There was shooting and bombing.

He saw cities lying in ruin. He saw rising seas sweeping across countries. And he saw huge storms blowing away vast forests and wiping out entire cities.

As the boy was barely 6 years old, it was a lot for his eyes to take in. So, one day, in utter despair, he took out his eyes and threw them in a lake.

Sometime later, a blind girl strolled down to the lake. The two eyes floated to the surface and told the girl to take them. So, she placed them in her face and began to see the most beautiful things—full rainbows and children laughing, flowers blooming and bees buzzing, trees touching the sky, birds singing and butterflies dancing.

One day the boy who threw away his eyes bumped into the girl with beautiful eyes. He told her his story and she told him hers. Then they wondered if she gave his eyes back to him, whether he would see the beautiful things she saw. So, she did it, and sure enough he saw all the beauty in the world that she knew. But, the strange thing was, even though she no longer had any eyes and was blind again, she did not lose sight of the beauty she had seen.

# Moses on the Mountain

Moses never came to the New World. He never sailed with Columbus, encountered an Indian, or tasted an apple pie. Not that he missed out, his hands quite full, plus all that legwork going up and down that mountain for those 10 Commandments.

According to legend passed on from the first settlers to the indigenous people they met, here is what really went down at Sinai…

Moses goes up the mountain where God hands him the commandments and tells him to say to the people he will protect and bless them forever if they obey these laws. Moses mumbles something under his breath, but goes down to the people, tells them what God promised, and reads the ten laws.

The people break into discussion groups for some time, then return with a list of counter proposals. One group doesn't like the first few laws about only one God and no images and the name in vain one. They think these laws are both unnecessary and egotistical. Another group thinks the one about not killing should be at the top and there should be one about parents respecting their children as well as the other way around. And so forth and so on.

After much haggling, Moses says hush, he'll go back up the mountain and negotiate some better laws. Tell Him to keep it simple, one person shouts. So, Moses goes back up to God, tells him what the people want, mentioning the simple part. God says the people are tough customers. Moses mumbles something.

Finally, God scribbles one thing on a new tablet, hands it to Moses, who takes it down to the people, and reads the one law. Always be grateful! There is a long silence. Then the people cheer their approval loud and clear, chanting, Thank you, Moses, Thank you, Moses, Thank you, Moses. Then, they decide to add an addendum to the law.

So, Moses, quite exhausted by now and out of breath, goes back up the mountain, where God asks him what the people said, to which Moses replies, they said to tell you, Thank you. They will always be grateful. But they reserve the right to renegotiate.

# The River of the Dancing Fishes

There once was a man who forgot where he was going. It was the strangest thing. One moment he was walking down a country road headed for an appointment and the next moment he completely forgot where he was going. So, he stopped, looked around, scratched his head, and decided to keep walking.

Sometime later he saw another man walking towards him. This other man seemed to sense his uncertainty, and so he stopped and he asked him if he was lost. No, I don't believe I am, said the first man, and the two men continued on their opposite ways. Farther down the road a woman approached him and asked if she could give him a hand. He thanked her politely, but assured her he didn't need a hand, and they wished each other a good day and that was that.

Much later, a young boy came down the road with a fishing pole, stopped and asked the man. Excuse me, sir, but do you know the way to the River of Dancing Fishes? I reckon I do, said the man, follow me. So, he led the boy down to the river where they sat on the bank and talked about life.

Life is like a river, said the man. It just keeps rolling along. I guess so, said the boy. Life is also like a road, the man offered. You just keep walking until you get where you are walking to. Suppose so, answered the boy, who, about to fish for the dancing fishes, stopped and said, By the way, Mister, was there someplace you were walking to before I interrupted you? The man looked at the boy, smiled, and replied. Clearly, I was walking down to the River of Dancing Fishes to have this enlightening conversation with you.

# The Sunflower Man

✕✕✕✕✕✕✕✕✕✕✕✕✕

Once there lived a man who loved sunflowers. It started in his own back yard where they grew magically. Then he felt motivated to share the joy all over the land. In just a few years, Kings County became a kingdom of sunflowers. The only problem was, these flowers were annuals, not perennials. So, the Sunflower Man made a deal with a local squirrel. He would supply the squirrel with an abundance of various seeds and berries, and the squirrel, in return, would redistribute the sunflower seeds every Fall for the following Spring.

So it was that the Sunflower man was able to create a huge array of sunflowers, endless fields of gold. It was a truly splendid sight to see, miles and miles of tall sunny, smiling beams of light. Of course, people came from all over the world to view the fields and snap countless photos with their little smart phones.

One day it all came to an end. A huge hurricane moved up the coast. They said it was a category 6 with winds over 200 miles per hour. They named it Apocalypse and it came steamrolling up the coast and down upon the Sunflower man and all the land. The winds, combined with the torrential rains and floods, wiped out everything that stood, uprooting huge maple trees and sending every last sunflower to utter oblivion.

When Apocalypse subsided, Sunflower Man fell to his knees in despair. As he wept, a solitary squirrel appeared with a seed in his mouth. Then another. And behind him a long line of faithfully marching little angels, each one with a little sunflower seed in his mouth, clearly keeping their part of the deal.

# The Prodigal Father

There lived a troubled man out by the ocean who loved to watch the waves come in. He was a lawyer by day and poet by night. He loved writing both legal briefs and sonnets. In many ways, he was blessed as he had a lovely wife, two fine children, and a quality of life many envied. But he was troubled.

He blamed his troubles on his son, calling him his prodigal son-of-a-bitch, not meaning to insult his wife. It was just the expression that fell from his lips. In the man's mind, his son had abandoned him, running off to some uppity university instead of attending the very respectable local college. It wasn't just the price tag that irked him. It was more the feeling that the life he had created for his family was not good enough for this kid. He had to go looking for something better.

So it was, he called his own son a prodigal son-of-a- bitch. The fact that his lovely wife supported the boy's decision to run off might have made the expression more accurate than he cared to admit. So, it came to pass that the wife died of a cancer in her breast, leaving the troubled man with a broken heart, alone and abandoned. The next day he received an invitation in the mail to attend his son's graduation. He felt torn between a genuine desire to go and celebrate his son's accomplishment and the bitterness he felt as a rejected father.

At the end of his rope, the troubled man went for a walk in the park, then crossed the street and entered the temple to talk to the rabbi, a man he knew as a friend as well as a spiritual advisor. He found himself sobbing in the rabbi's office, explaining his woes and especially the neglect from his son. The rabbi, a very kind man, listened patiently without interrupting. After, they sat in silence and prayed for an answer.

Finally, the rabbi said this. Do you want to hear what I have to say? Yes, of course. I believe it is you who have abandoned your son. You let

Bob Mandel

him go out into the world without a father to guide him. He went to a fancy university in another borough. Big deal. You can afford it. What you cannot afford is the price of being a prodigal father. The troubled man looked into the eyes of the Rabbi, and nodded.

# The Pheasant

〰〰〰〰〰〰〰〰〰

There once was a beautiful pheasant who thought he was a turkey. He lived in New World Park and was quite dashing. This is what happened.

One fine morning the pheasant was walking by himself when he came across a mother and her twelve baby turkeys marching behind her. So, the pheasant fell in line behind the last baby turkey and followed. At a certain point the mother noticed the mistaken bird and tried to shoo him away, but he was a persistent fellow and caused no harm so the mother decided to ignore him.

Sometime later the mother went off and left her children with the pheasant, who by that time had become a trusted baby sitter. When the mother failed to return, the pheasant went to the front of the line and led the babies on a long march, searching for the mother. Eventually, they found her frolicking with a gobbler, a handsome tom. The mother, quite flustered at the interruption, and the gobbler, not liking it one bit, chased off the pheasant telling him he didn't belong and should be with his own kind.

So, the pheasant went away and walked by himself for many days. Then he came across a family of ducks. They were swimming in a pond, the mother followed by her five little ducklings. So, the pheasant dived into the pond and dutifully took his place behind the last little baby duck.

So it was that the pheasant who thought he was a turkey came to believe he was a duck.

# The Woman Who Was Up in the Air

〰〰〰〰〰〰〰〰〰〰

A woman was up in the air. She didn't know what to think. On the one hand, everything seemed normal, her husband, two kids, dog and cat not behaving abnormally, but on the other hand, something was up. So, she was up in the air.

It started one morning when her husband woke up, turned over in bed, placed a finger on his nose, and then went off to his office without a word. Then her son and daughter ate their breakfast in silence, left the dishes on the table, and went off to school. The dog and the cat both shook their heads and scooted out into the yard, not even begging for treats. Something was up.

So, the woman was up in the air. Later that day all hell broke loose. The rain came pouring down. The kids came home screaming and crying. The husband stormed in complaining. And the dog and cat came slithering in, trying to stay invisible.

So, it was the woman who was up in the air asked each of her loved ones what was what, her husband telling her his job sucked, her kids echoed the same sentiment about school, and the dog and the cat nodded in complete agreement. And when the woman considered her own life, suck was not a bad description. Thus, they all agreed they were not one happy family.

So, the woman who was up in the air had an idea. That night she made a big party. She invited all the neighbors, as she noticed the entire block was not one big happy neighborhood. She called it the great blast of the disgruntled whiners and complainers. Thus, it came to be that all the miserable folk came together to air it out.

# The Incarcerated Woman

Once there was an incarcerated woman who lived over by the park. Why or who had incarcerated her were unknown. Perhaps she did it to herself. She just woke up one morning in a fog of incarceration and time drifted on. She tried to keep her mind busy, meditating, studying, and praying for liberation, but incarceration kept her locked up. It was a tough prison and she saw no way out.

Then, one day, something changed. The incarcerated woman looked out the windows of her mind and saw a flicker of light. To be sure, bars still defined her windows, but at least there was a glimmer of hope. In the glimmer she saw a glow. In the glow stood a huge bowl of light, and within that bowl of light something amazing happened. A goat came to her. He threw a rope and she grabbed it. He told her to tie it around her waist which she did.

And so, she became tethered in a bowl of light. Then the goat pulled and pulled and ever so slowly he pulled her out of her incarceration, dragging the bowl and her slowly through a valley, across a river, and towards a distant mountain.

After a very long haul, they arrived at the top of a mountain and the goat asked her what she had learned from her ordeal. She looked down the mountain and saw endless fields of golden grains and flowers. Then she turned to the goat and tears welled in her eyes. Thank you, she said. Thank you so much. I never felt so free until you tethered me.

# Autumn Joy

⸻⟨⟩⟨⟩⟨⟩⟨⟩⟨⟩⟨⟩⟨⟩⸻

There lived an elderly man, all alone, out in the boondocks. Without family or friends, he was a hermit, his only love a little garden out back. Long ago, he had divided it into four quadrants, one for each season. Thus, he had his daffodils for Spring, his dahlias for Summer, and his Autumn Joy, a variety of sedum. Finally, he had his Winter spot, a Zen garden of little round stones he raked while waiting for his Spring flowers to grow.

One year it came to pass that his Autumn Joy did not bloom, and then again the next year. As they often did not arrive until October, the old man was quite patient, but after the third year he lost hope. At the end of his rope, he heard about a woman they called the Garden Witch who lived over the border in Queensland and was said to have a knack for seemingly dead plants.

So, he rang her up and she came over to offer her opinion of the fate of his Autumn Joy. No Spring chicken herself, she mumbled to herself while running her jagged fingers through her wild red hair. He asked her what had gone wrong with her hands and she told him how that wicked carpal tunnel syndrome had taken all the feeling from her fingers and how she now communicated with the plants with whispers and sighs. So, she went to work, bending over the clusters of what should have been Autumn Joy but what seemed to the naked eye like dead sprays, and began whispering her incantations, humming her little ditties, and breathing her sighs upon the lost souls. As he closed his eyes, listening to her sweet sounds and kind whispers, he began to lose himself in her magic, she taking his breath away, even so late in life. When he opened his eyes, he found himself sitting in his Zen Garden, the red- headed witch smiling at him.

Come along, dear, she said to him. We've done all the good we can do today. Let's give your little princesses a few days to decide what they have in mind. So, she took him by his hand, gnarly though hers were, and they went into his house for a cup of tea and some biscuits, so to say. The next morning when they came downstairs and walked out to the garden, the Joy of Autumn had popped.

# The Woman Who Faced Death

There once lived a woman on Death Row at a famous prison on an island in the middle of nowhere. She had been convicted of drowning her twin toddlers in a lake, notwithstanding her lame defense that she couldn't swim so how could she have rescued them. The fact was she threw her own two children off a rowboat with her own two hands, several witnesses testifying.

So it was, she spent her last days of her current lifetime face-to-face with Death, discussing a wide range of topics, not the least of which was what she could expect once he took her away for good. Dismissing the traditional notions of heaven and hell, he put it to her this way. When you come with me once and for all, it's somewhat like a marriage, only not the kind till death do you part, if you catch my drift. It really depends on what we make of it, mostly what you make of it since my job is mainly to never let go of your hand.

The woman sat there, thinking about the words of Death, and then replied. So, you're saying that when you scoop me off, I must submit to you as in traditional wedlock, and then it's up to me to make the marriage work? Death nodded and smiled kindly. More or less. It sounds like a one-way street, she replied. More or less, he repeated. Well, as you compare the arrangement to a regular marriage where the man always has the upper hand, what if I reject your proposal completely? Death shook his head. Can't do that, he said. The clock is ticking. Think of it as a prearranged marriage. There is no escape.

And thus, several days later, she marched to her execution without uttering another word. As she passed over, she saw herself walking down an aisle, Death waiting for her, a regular wedding ceremony with a choir of angels and a priest presiding. Later that night, when Death came to her for the final consummation, she turned to him and said to him, smiling. Sorry, my dear.

I feel a terrible migraine coming on.

# The Gatherer

Once there was a boy who loved to gather. He gathered all things, collecting them in piles and hiding them in secret places. He gathered stones, he gathered sticks, he gathered nuts, and he gathered berries, taking great joy in his enterprise. He had secret hiding places in the park where he stored his troves.

One day a girl asked him to help her gather flowers. He agreed and so they walked through the gardens gathering beautiful flowers. They came to a small house where a little boy lived. His mother was gone. The boy said he had nothing, but they were welcome to come in. So, the boy who loved to gather and the girl entered the house, looked around, and, seeing nothing, gave the boy who had nothing the flowers and went home.

The next day the boy who loved to gather gathered all his stones and carried them in a sack over his shoulder to the boy who had nothing and left the stones in front of the small house. The following day, he brought his sticks, and then his nuts and berries. So it was that the boy who had nothing came to receive abundance from a stranger, his new friend, who loved to gather and give.

Much later, one day, the boy found a cave. He entered. Inside was an old man sitting by a pile of gold. In fact, he was sifting sand through an enormous sieve which turned the sand into gold. Wow, exclaimed the boy. Wow, replied the old man. What shall we do with all this gold? I've got an idea, said the boy.

Bob Mandel

# The Man Who Took His Chances

⋄⋄⋄⋄⋄⋄⋄⋄⋄⋄⋄⋄⋄⋄⋄

A man was driving through the desert when his car broke down. He got out, looked under the hood, could not figure out what had gone wrong, checked again, and saw he had just run out of gas. How stupid could he have been, driving across a desert without filling up his tank! So, thinking he was quite stupid, he waited for help but no one came along.

The sun was strong, there was no shade, and the man had no water. Later, a rattlesnake approached and said to the man. I can take you out of your misery now or you can wait for the sun to do the dirty deed. I'll take my chances, the man said. The snake slithered off.

The next morning, the sun rose early and the man was in bad shape. A pack of coyotes approached and the leader said, we can take you out of your misery now or you can wait for the sun or the rattlesnake to do the dirty deed. I'll take my chances, the man said again, and the coyotes went away.

The next day, the sun was at its peak, the man was standing delirious under its deadly heat, and a beautiful woman drove by in a red Porsche. She passed him by, but then turned around, pulled up next to him, rolled down her window, and said. I can take you out of your misery now or you can stand there and wait for the sun, the rattlesnake or the coyotes to put an end to your misery. He looked at her, smiled, and said, Thank you, darling, but I much prefer for you to do the dirty deed.

# The Girl Who Dances with Rain

A girl is dancing with rain. She is so much in harmony with the rain she becomes the rain. She descends into the earth, watering the roots of trees and plants, herbs, and flowers. Coming to an underground lake, she floats to a stream and flows into a river, feeding the forests and then the green valley where workers gather the crops.

Later, the river empties into a sea and the girl becomes a warm current carrying her to tropical water. Beautiful rainbow fish swim around her, over and under and through her and she takes a deep breath, lets it go, and evaporates into the air above the rain forest where she becomes a cloud. She floats across the sky and becomes a Summer thunderstorm rolling over the fields, raining herself on the farmland below, feeding the corn, the wheat, and the vegetables. Dancing with rain, she sinks into the earth and enters a well deep down, where she becomes water for a local rancher, who brings her up in a bucket and makes himself a cup of morning coffee, sipping the girl who dances with the rain.

# The Anomaly Who Wake Up

A woman suddenly deviated from her usual position. She was a true anomaly. Her life usually proceeded in a predictable orbit. She'd wake up in the morning, make breakfast for her husband and the kids, send them off to do their usual business, and then get ready to face her day as a psychiatric social worker dealing with a variety of mental illnesses. She thought she loved her husband, believed her kids were the best, and always said her work was a calling from deep in her heart.

Then, one day, she became an anomaly. Or maybe she was always an anomaly and just realized it. She couldn't tell you exactly how it happened, but she had gone back to bed for a catnap before heading out to the clinic when the next thing she knew she found herself all alone in the middle of nowhere. She sat down and thought about her life for a very long time. She came to the realization that she was in the middle of nowhere, that her entire life was a fraud, and that she, her husband, and the kids were a family of zombies sleepwalking through life like the walking dead.

Oh, my God, she said to herself. Oh, my God! How could I have been so blind? When no answer came to her, she began to pray, which was most odd as she was not really a believer and never remembered praying before. But there she was in the middle of nowhere, praying for deliverance from her zombie life. Please, God. Please, God. Please, God. She repeated the words, a mantra with no sense, and she drifted further and further into herself, detaching altogether from her known world, which just yesterday was the only world she knew.

When she awakened, there she was, on a Bridge of Light, side by side with fellow travelers, all the Anomalies seeking a new life, all of whom seemed suddenly familiar, heading from a trajectory they had repeated over and over to a New and Unknown World that was calling them.

# The Rich Man and His Wife

◇◇◇◇◇◇◇◇◇◇◇◇◇

There once was a very rich man looking for a good wife. He lived in a castle and, as he wanted to be certain his wife would be a good woman, he devised a few questions to ask during the interview process. The questions were these. One, would you want to marry me if I were not so rich? Two, would you stay with me even if I lost all my money? And three, will you be frugal and manage my money scrupulously?

So, the first prospect enters his office. She is lovely, graceful, and smiles coyly. She answers yes to all three questions. He dismisses her, knowing she is lying. A second prospect arrives. She too is pleasing in appearance and bats her eyelashes in a certain way. When he poses the questions, she answers no to the first question and yes to the second and third ones. He sighs deeply, then dismisses her, knowing she is only pretending to be honest by being one third honest.

A third lady appears, nothing special to look at, but emanating a sweetness and warmth. She looks at him with an open face and answers no to all three questions. So, he marries her, knowing she is an honest woman.

Years pass and one day an economic crisis comes and the man tells his wife he has lost all his money. His good wife leaves him as she said she would.

Some years later, the man recovers his vast fortune, and his wife appears at his doorstep. Why have you returned, he asks? Because, she replies, I married you because you were rich, I left you when you were poor, and I am sorry, please forgive me, but I just cannot be frugal and manage your finances scrupulously.

Bob Mandel

# The Big Hand

There once was a woman who felt down in the dumps. Stuck in the boondocks, she was in the middle of her life and in a tailspin of poor me. Her husband was a drunkard, her two teenage boys were constantly flirting with the law, and her parents were always complaining, ungrateful and manipulative. She herself had been a schoolteacher for the last ten years, but she had completely lost her enthusiasm with both the lesson plans and the students, who seemed overnight to have turned from sweet to sour. Thus, it was she felt down in the dumps out in the boondocks.

She began searching for a new way. She went to a Life Coach who tried to motivate her, but she felt listless after each session. She tried a yoga class, but felt frustrated by how rigid was her once nimble body had become. She even went to a traditional psychologist who prescribed anti-depressants, which only depressed her more.

Finally, one day, she stood on top of a white cliff overlooking a black sea, ready to do the dastardly deed. Put an end to it all, she heard a voice in her mind say, but immediately afterwards another voice countered, don't do something you might regret and cannot reverse. She couldn't make up her mind either way when a huge gust of wind picked her up and threw her into the air. That mighty gust carried her clear across the sky to another world.

When she landed, she was a bit dizzy, but no worse for wear, and when she looked around for what had pushed her so far and so high, she saw a big hand. Who are you, she asked? I'm your Big Hand, the hand replied. Everyone has one. Really? Really. Usually, we're Unseen Hands, but I thought I'd make myself visible this once. Why did you push me, Big Hand? Well, clearly, you were going to jump, so I wanted to make sure your jump became a leap.

# Father Time

There came a day when Father Time decided he would retire. After what seemed like an eternity of directing traffic on the super highway of life, age had finally caught up with him. I've had it, he declared to all his associates and underlings. I have sat up here and watched all things come and pass, shuffle by me, slow, fast, and faster. I have heard it all about change, progress, evolution and development. But from my particular point of view, I can't see it. Maybe Time is blind, I can't say, but I think I need time out.

At first, the brethren objected, arguing that without Father Time life itself could not continue. It was his mission to lead the way for all of eternity. Even his sweet son, the dreamy eyed Little Tic Toc begged. But daddy, you should not get so down in the dumps because of a mere few million years of failure. But Father Time would hear none of it. Nope, he replied. Nope nope nope nope. What's done is done, no turning back. I'm plum tired and that's that.

Thus, it was that nobody said a word for a very long time. In fact, it seemed like time had stopped. Actually, it had. Father Time's retirement had the immediate effect of stopping all time, right there and then, like a train roaring down the tracks and screeching to an abrupt thumping halt. Only a silent, smoky chugging in place.

Finally, well, after some time would have passed had there still been time, Father Time's brother, the beloved Uncle Now, the Master of the Moment, rolled up his sleeves and chirped in. Well, folks, I guess that leaves me as next in line to take over, that is, if there are no objections.

So it was that Father Time took a walk in the woods and Uncle Now twiddled his thumbs, and not much happened. The world below grew restless and unhappy. The angels above cracked their knuckles and worried. Time would have passed if it could move, but it just stayed stuck like that train going nowhere.

Then it happened that Father Time returned from his walk and said, what's new? Everyone shrugged their shoulders in unison, whereupon Father Time coughed three times into his hands, then rubbed them together and declared, I reckon the rumors I started about my retirement were a bit premature. No doubt about it. Time to get things moving again. Can't just stand around like a bunch of ignoramuses picking our noses and scratching our arses all day! And so it was that the train stalled down below blasted its horn, cranked up its steam and got chugging and then rolling down those rickety-rackety rails of endless time.

# The Boy Who
# Learned Kindness

◇◇◇◇◇◇◇◇◇◇◇◇◇◇◇

A young boy from a prairie town wanted to learn kindness. He knew it was an important quality and was trying his best to understand it. He interviewed all sorts of smart adults for their opinions on the subject. His history teacher said it meant being a good person, but that seemed too general an answer. His basketball coach said it meant being a good team-mate, but the boy knew it was more than about basketball. His father said it meant being generous, and that sounded pretty good but not quite right either. Finally, his mother said, well, son, you'll just have to find out for yourself, and he knew that was the truth.

So, the young boy set out to find kindness for himself. The first thing he decided to do was offer his seat in the front of the school bus to the blind girl.

Next, he offered a helping hand to every elderly person crossing a street. Then, he stayed late after class every day to clean up the library, after which he carried the librarian's heavy bag to her car. All these good deeds made the young man learn about kindness, but one thing really taught him more than anything else.

One day he was riding his bicycle without a care in the world when a car came along and nearly killed him. He lay in the street, eyes closed, both legs broken, a bloody mess. Then, all the people coming, the blind girl, elderly folk, librarian, basketball coach, all his teammates, classmates, history teacher, and of course, his mom and dad. In fact, the whole town came running in a massive display of simple old human kindness. The boy opened his eyes, smiled, and said, Oh My God.

# The Girl with Two Left Feet

Down by the railroad tracks, a girl with two left feet struggled to belong. Not that she stood out in a crowd or anything. In fact, she was neither clumsy nor awkward, and, if you didn't know her true disability, you might have called her agile and graceful.

Nevertheless, in her own mind her condition inhibited her, so she avoided the dance floor at all costs, and participating in any kind of sports activities was out of the question. This, despite the fact that everyone in her whole school knew she was the fastest thing on two legs, including the boys, and if she weren't so self-conscious, she would have been the cross-country champion of the entire city, state, and perhaps nation. Shy as she was, the girl with two left feet grew up in the shadows, excelling at academics, preferring to exercise her brain muscles than the other kind.

Time passed. Though she tried to remain invisible, she could not hide the fact that she was growing into a very beautiful young lady and there was no way for the boys not to notice. Little by little, they began to approach her, invite her to parties, movies, or just a walk in the park, all of which she summarily rejected.

Until there came a day when a certain young man, who had a certain gait about him and a sparkle in his eyes, implored her to walk with him in the Botanical Gardens. She was about to brush him off but somehow said yes instead of no, and the following Saturday she found herself enchanted by the flowers as well as the feller.

As they walked that day and many following ones, they discovered they had much in common, both their academic interests and their distaste for dancing and athletics. They graduated at the top of their class, attended the same university, following which the charming young man popped the question to the girl with two left feet, who promptly accepted.

Their wedding night, the beautiful bride, throwing caution to the wind, stripped bare and revealed her two left feet. She literally had the two of them. Whereupon the handsome groom, not to be outdone, showed his as she had shown hers, and, lo and behold, he had two right feet. They practically laughed their heads off, but couldn't take their eyes off each other's feet. In fact, they spent the whole night playing footsie. And so it was, the next morning, they decided they were a match made in Heaven, as together they had the right number of both feet.

# The Humidor

A man is showing his son his precious humidor, which he inherited from his own father, who was given it by his grandfather in Kiev. It is ceramic, hand-painted, with images of crusading knights. The boy is captivated by the humidor. His father explains that he keeps three Cuban cigars in it. When he finishes smoking them, he uses the humidor to save money for three new stogies, one dollar a day for forty-five days.

So, you don't smoke for forty-five days? Yes, you know I do, but only the Dominican ones, which are much cheaper. The boy takes in all this knowledge, not that he has the slightest desire ever to smoke cigars. His father motions for him to follow, so they go to a closet where his dad rummages, coming out with another humidor. They sit side-by-side on the bed and the father hands the humidor to his son. It is identical to the first one. I saved this one, the twin, for you. The boy, overwhelmed with gratitude, does not know what to say. I know you may never smoke cigars, which would not be a bad thing, but you can use it to save money for something you really want, such as a baseball bat, roller skates, or even a new bicycle.

So it is, the boy begins to save money, nickels, dimes, quarters, and an occasional dollar, sacrificing an ice cream cone or even a Saturday double feature at the local movie house, all for the pleasure of collecting money in the humidor which the crusaders protect.

Time passes until one day his dad asks him what he is saving for and when he will have enough money to buy it. The boy smiles and tells his dad it's a secret. The next morning, the boy brings his humidor around the block to the smoke shop, empties the money in front of the cash register, and buys his dad three Montecristo Cuban cigars.

# The Lost Man

‹◇◇◇◇◇◇◇◇◇◇◇◇◇›

Back in the last century a man lost his mind and drifted without direction. This man was no bum, but he might as well have been one, not knowing who in God's name he was. It was a strange story. One night he went to bed, his mind in perfect working order, and the next morning when he woke up, poof, it was gone. He could not remember who he was, where he was, or what he was supposed to do with his life. He just sat on the edge of his bed and tried to make sense of his situation. Nothing came to him.

So, he got up, went downstairs to the kitchen, opened the refrigerator and took a gulp of milk from the bottle. Then a thought came to him. Cows. So, he went outside and sure enough there were cows everywhere. Farm, he said to himself. Must be a farmer. So, he took care of the cows for a few days until a man came along who said it was his farm, told the man who lost his mind to go away, it was not his job to be a farmer.

So, the man went away. The next morning, he woke up and he was sitting in front of a big desk with a globe on it. He was wearing a suit and tie and talking to a group of people about new sources of sustainable energy. Someone came up to him and told him he was at the wrong meeting; this was a cruise ship company and he should go away. He did.

He woke up the next morning in a boxcar on a freight train. A hobo came up to him and asked, who are you? I don't know, the man replied. Well, then, the hobo said. You're on the right train. We are all a bunch of don't know whos on our way to who knows where in order to do God knows what.

# The Giant Ladybug

Once there was a giant Ladybug. She lived in a remote part of the land where people were tiny like ants and bugs were bigger than them. One day the giant Ladybug was crawling slowly across a field when she spotted a family of little people in the miniature backyard near a sweet little house. She observed them from a distance. She saw the little daddy grilling something on the barbecue, the mommy and toddler picking little tomatoes from the garden, and two boys throwing a ball back and forth. She thought they were so cute that she gathered them up, took them home and put them in a glass jar, poking little holes in the lid so they could breathe.

Later that day, the giant Ladybug's mom came home from her place of work, noticed the little people in the jar, and scolded her daughter for removing the humans from their natural habitat. So, the Giant Ladybug obeyed her mom and returned the little people to the place she found them.

But the family of humans was not the same. They were so shaken up by their ordeal that they could not sleep, plus they had many post-traumatic stress symptoms such as headaches, indigestion, hypertension, and panic attacks. As the Giant Ladybug continued to observe her pet humans, she became anxiety-ridden, seeing their various ailments. So, she went to her friend, the Wise Old Owl who, seeing what havoc the Giant Ladybug had wreaked, cast a spell to calm her nerves, whereupon the ladybug began shrinking in size until all her giantness was gone and she was reduced to an ordinary little bug. Then the owl ate her.

# God's Epiphany

One day God had an epiphany. He was weeding his garden, one of his favorite pastimes in Heaven, when a light bulb flashed on and off in his mind, always a sign of a thought worthy of attention. This flickering light was a kind of Morse Code from the Infinite, giving God the guidance even He needed. The more he thought about this particular message from the light bulb, the more he thought it was a really good idea. So, he did it.

And this was the epiphany. He would gather all the people down below and tell them they had a special assignment and that was to clean up the whole planet, get rid of all the garbage in the air and sea, do a massive recycling, eliminate fossil fuels, and drastically simplify their life style. And when they completed this assignment, he would give them the most wonderful reward in the universe.

So, the people listened to God's epiphany and they thought it was an offer they couldn't refuse, and they set about taking care of all that he requested. When they had finished the project and the Earth looked brand new, fresh as the day of Creation, they gathered before God again and waited to receive their well-deserved reward. God looked down at them benevolently, his beautiful children on Planet Earth, smiled and said. Now, my children, now that you have cleaned up your mess, see the world as it was meant to be in all its beauty and glory. Behold Paradise Now.

# The Cousins

﹡﹡﹡﹡﹡﹡﹡﹡﹡﹡﹡﹡

Two men are walking in opposite directions when they bump into each other. They look at each other, then again, and also a third time. One is tall and lean, the other short and stocky. Where you headed, cousin?, asks the tall one. Nowhere in particular, the short one replies. Just walking down the road. What about you, cousin? Well, my truck broke down back up the road there so I'm headed for the gas station to find a repairman. No need for that. I can give you a helping hand. I'd be much obliged, says the tall one.

So, they head up the road where they find the broken-down truck. The short one opens the hood while the tall one tries to start the engine but it won't turn over. The short one gets under the truck and seems to know what he's doing. Then he goes back to look under the hood and fiddles around some more. Finally, he tells the tall one, start her up, cousin. So, the tall one turns the key and sure enough, she fires up real fine. Wow, cousin, you sure got the touch. I am deeply in your debt. Not at all, replies the short one. In fact, I thank you for the opportunity to put my service to good use. Well, says the tall one, leaning out the window, be that as it might be, is there anywhere I can drive you? Well, cousin, you're very kind to offer, replies the short one, especially seeing how we never laid eyes on each other before. But I reckon I'll just keep walking and see if I bump into any other cousins in need.

# The Rabbi

There was a ver y famous rabbi in the New World whose congregation was large and prosperous. In fact, he didn't even look Jewish as he was plump, jovial, with a long white beard. They called him the Jewish Santa Claus.

He was a very wise man named Rabbi Kinderman. He loved children and had twelve grandchildren of his own, to whom he would listen and tell stories every Saturday. He called them his tribe, his twelve apostles, and his precious angels. So, it was a very great tragedy when one of those precious angels, Michael by name, died of a mysterious disease. The entire family grieved for a very long time. The whole congregation joined in the feeling of loss. Even the mayor of the city and his family paid a condolence call. They buried the child in a small cemetery out by the bay.

In time, the pain subsided and Rabbi Kinderman seemed to return to his good old jovial self. He continued to instruct children in the teachings of the sacred scriptures, enjoying spinning the old stories into magical tales children could understand. For instance, when he told the story of Noah, he changed the ark to a ferry and had Noah gathering all the animals from the local zoo, then embarking on a long journey from the docks across the river to a neighboring town. That's the kind of rabbi Kinderman was.

One cold Winter Saturday before dawn, the rabbi went to visit the grave of his precious angel Michael. He placed some flowers, sunflowers at the foot of the headstone, sat on the grass, dropped his head and began sobbing. Then, he spoke, saying these words. Oh, Michael. I don't know how long I can go on. My heart is so broken into ten thousand pieces or more. I speak of joy and hope, but I do not walk my words. My love is empty without you to fill my cup. Oy, Michael, Michael, I fear I will take my life to join you.

At that very moment, a big wind swirled around the grave site and the rabbi. The sound of a happy child could be heard in the swirling. And, presto pronto, there was the precious little angel Michael, hovering above his own grave, smiling. The rabbi looked up. Michael? Yes, Grandpa. Here I am, happy as a clam. So why do you suffer when I am so happy? Rejoice. I am with God every day now. He tells stories almost as good as yours. And, guess what, Grandpa? God is also with you every day. If you listen carefully, he is talking to you right now.

# The Most Beautiful Woman in the World

She was the most beautiful woman in the world. She lived uptown, but the whole city was abuzz with her. You could feel her from a mile away. She'd come walking down the street and, as if preceded by a parade of heralding angels, space itself would part and her beauty would come shining forth, announcing her imminent arrival. And then she would be there, beauty in plain sight, all the world waving from the sidewalks, snapping photos, seeking selfies with her, and falling over themselves from the power of such beauty.

Meanwhile, even as she waved in appreciation and gratitude for the lovely attention, the most beautiful woman in the world could not understand all the fuss. When she returned home every evening, she would say to her husband, son and daughter, I don't see why they all think I'm so beautiful. They must be blind out of their minds. They, in turn, would roll their eyes, throw their hands up in the air, and tell her she was the blind one.

So it was that one evening she went to her trusty mirror, where she made herself up every morning, saying to her image. I just don't see it. Her reflection winked, shrugged her shoulders, bent over, and whispered. You need a shrink.

So, she found a psychiatrist, who, dumbstruck by her beauty, almost fainted before gathering his senses and asking her what he could do for her. She explained her dilemma. He listened, then responded. Clearly, you do not feel beautiful inside. So, when you look in the mirror, you see your inner flaws instead of your outer beauty. You mean, she replied, I have an ugly soul? Not exactly, he said, giggling a bit. You only think your soul is ugly and that is what clouds your vision. I can send you to my friend, the shaman down the street and he can set you straight.

So, the most beautiful woman in the world visited the shaman down the street, who performed some wizardry, as it were, and, turning the woman inside out, set her straight indeed. When she returned home and looked in the mirror, she saw the most beautiful woman in the world. Her reflection gave her a thumbs up. The only problem was that her husband, two kids, and all the locals no longer turned their heads when she appeared. Of course, they continued to recognize her undeniable beauty, but now it was an internal beauty hidden beneath an ordinary exterior. Meanwhile, all the heralding angels went looking for a new parade.

# The People Who Forgot

There once was a time when almost everyone in the entire kingdom and perhaps all the world forgot who they were. This is what happened. A little boy woke up one morning to discover his parents forgot they were his parents and that they were husband and wife. Worst of all, they completely forgot they were even people. He tried to remind them, but they said to forget it. Then he went outside and all the neighborhood was the same, completely forgetful that they were people and that he was a wonderful little boy they always smiled at, tipped their hats when they saw him, and told him to have a beautiful day. They didn't remember a darn thing.

This went on for several days until one day the little boy woke up and discovered his parents had vanished completely and instead, two mice were scurrying about the kitchen and enjoying the contents of the refrigerator. When he asked the mice where his parents had gone, they twitched their ears and devoured a chunk of cheese.

So, the boy went outside and discovered, where his neighborhood had been, now spread a prairie full of grazing sheep. The little boy asked a sheep where all his neighbors had gone, to which the sheep replied with a loud BAA three times.

The boy, totally confused by now, headed down to the local zoo where he discovered two elephants bathing in a pond. Thus, he asked an elephant. Wise Sir, do you know what has become of my parents and my neighbors because all I see now are two mice in my house and sheep roaming outside? The wise old elephant spun his trunk in the air and replied. Well, I reckon they all forgot who they were and so they became who they were not. The little boy considered this new information, and then began to cry. Well, what about me, he said. What's going to become of me? Whereupon the wise old elephant responded, Well, I suppose you have two choices. You can either forget who you are and become one of them mice or sheep. Or, you can remember you are a fine little boy and grow up to be a fine human being.

# The Disagreeable Couple

Once there was a couple from the flatlands who disagreed about everything. And this is not a story about two people who agree to disagree. In the case of these two disagreeable people, they could never even agree to anything. So, it was they were doomed to opposition until one day they were forced to confront a common opponent.

This is the way it went down. Every Summer the couple vacationed up either in the northernmost mountains and or down in the tropics, since they could never agree on one place. One fine day, while hiking a trail up a gentle, green mountain, he behind her so as not to affront her, each of them mumbling under their breaths, they simultaneously heard a loud blast and looked up where they observed a huge dam bursting and the river rising rapidly, soon about to overflow its banks. Looking at each other, he took her hand, she pulled it away, and they ran for cover.

They came to a cave and thought they had found shelter, so they ducked in, but the waters kept rising and pretty soon they knew they needed to seek higher ground. So, taking her by her hand again, she pulling away again, they hurried up the mountain, the river continuing to rise behind them. When they reached the top, they were out of breath but the water was still climbing and snaking around them. So, standing there, on the peak, the rushing river seeming to reach for them, the man turned to the woman and said, Can we at least agree on this one thing? I mean, here we are with no place to go, right? Whereupon she looked at him, shook her head, shouted, NO, and then promptly jumped into the river. He took a deep breath and, without second thought, dived in after her.

Two days later, they were found on the bank of the river, still breathing, holding hands, and apologizing profusely for the time they had wasted in petty disputes.

# The True Friend

~~~~~~~~~~~~~~~~~~~~~~~~~~~~~~~~~~~~

There once lived a man who knew the truth. He could smell a lie whenever it came near him. For example, one time a girl told him she loved him more than anyone in the world and he knew she was just making that up. Sure enough, a couple of weeks later she picked up and ran off with another feller. Then there was the occasion when his cousin asked to borrow some money and promised he'd pay it back in a month. The man who knew the truth knew his cousin was lying, but he gave him the money anyway because, well, it was his cousin.

So, it came to pass he met this stranger and they hit it off from day one. They went fishing and bowling, and chewed the fat at the local watering hole. One day this stranger, fast becoming a good friend, turned, and said, I reckon I'm gonna be your best friend forever. Well, our man knew a made-up fable when it was looking at him, so he just shook his head and walked away, and never talked to that man again.

One day, years later, the man who knew the truth was accused of a murder he did not commit and there was a regular trial. And just as it seemed our truth-telling man might get put away due to a pack of lies, his former best friend for life appeared, gave him a phony alibi, and he got off scot free.

Later, the two friends were shooting the breeze when the truthful one said to the one who lied for him. You know, friend, I owe you an apology. When you said you were my best friend for life, I thought you were fibbing. But now that you lied to save my life, I know it was the God's honest truth.

Bob Mandel

# The Great Ring of Fire

Once there was a Ring of Fire that appeared out by Landsend, a great circle of flames in the sky, its base almost touching the ground. Anything that passed through the Ring would never be the same again because the Fire changed everything. A black cat jumping became a golden eagle soaring. A vulture, a butterfly. Even a bunch of helium balloons drifted lazily under and became a flock of Canadian geese. From a distance the Ring resembled a gigantic hula hoop of fire spinning in the sky.

One day a young boy was observing the huge hoop when he noticed a spark fly off towards him and drop right down plop on his head. Sort of like the apple that struck Sir Isaac Newton. Only this spark was not about gravity, but about metamorphosis. If the Ring of Fire transformed everything that passed through it, the boy thought, maybe people could throw all their bad things through it and the bad things would become good things.

So the boy began by climbing up a huge tree and throwing an old pair of worn-out sneakers through the burning hoop and when he climbed down and went to see where they landed, lo and behold, he picked up a fine new pair of cowboy boots, his very size.

Encouraged by his experiment, he told his parents who were skeptical at first, but when he showed them by climbing back up the tree and tossing his dad's broken Timex watch which came out the other side as a true Rolex, his dad was mightily impressed.

So, he told his neighbors, who in turn told their relatives, and so it was the whole neighborhood began throwing their old stuff through the Ring of Fire, old toasters becoming new microwaves, old cells phones emerging as the latest iPhones, and then even old TVs, washing machines, and, yes, old beat-up jalopy cars (heaved through the giant hoop with the help of a huge catapult) landing on their spanking new Michelins as Mercedes, Porsches, and even Roll Royces.

Now, it just so happened that the little boy with the spark had a friend who was not so good. One night, when nobody was looking, he began to throw stones through the ring and they came out the other side as gold nuggets. He collected a lot of gold over many nights, but a strange thing started to happen. The Ring of Fire grew weaker and weaker. Nobody knew why until one morning the good boy found his friend with the gold. He told him how bad it was and how he was killing the fire. So, together they threw all the nuggets back the other way, returning them to stones and restoring the fire to its good use.

One day the little boy felt a new array of sparks strike his head and he told his father, who told the borough president, who told the mayor who told the governor himself. Thus, it happened that a new project was born and prisoners from the penitentiary jumped through the ring and came out as good Samaritans, alcoholics passed through squeaky clean, and even the old and the sick were lifted through the Ring of Fire, rejuvenated and healed.

Many years passed, the Ring grew older, its fire dimmer, but the little boy, now a wise old shaman, captured yet one more spark, and rolling it in the palms of his hands, held the remnant of the magical Ring of Fire and flung it high up into the starry starry night where it exploded into a magnificent new planet.

Bob Mandel

# *Love and Hate*

◇◇◇◇◇◇◇◇◇◇◇◇◇◇◇

Once upon a time three wise women entered a village suffering from a rare illness. Everyone was saying the opposite of what they wanted to say. For example, the grocer wanted to tell his wife, Good morning, my beloved, but what came out instead was, Go to Hell, you witch. Also, the school marm wanted to say to her students, How are my little munchkins this morning? But what came out instead was, What misery will you dirty little rascals cause me today? And this is just a small sampling.

So, the three wise women each offered a remedy. The first one said, well, the solution was quite simple. When each person spoke, he should immediately say, I'm sorry, what I meant to say, and then say the exact opposite thing. So, the people tried that, but it didn't work because when they tried to say the opposite, what came out was the opposite of the opposite, namely the same old mean thing.

Wise Woman #2 then suggested they begin their communication by saying, Don't believe a word I'm about to say, but..." That sounded clever but in practice was a disaster because people didn't believe they should believe they shouldn't believe.

Finally, Wise Woman #3 said. This is all rubbish. It's clear you all really hate each other and have pushed it down for too many years. So just tell each the truth. Say how you feel. So it was, the entire village appeared to be healed as everyone paraded around, saying how they felt.

# The Origin of Nature

⟨⟩⟨⟩⟨⟩⟨⟩⟨⟩⟨⟩⟨⟩⟨⟩

A long time ago a Wizard, Witch, and Shaman gathered to discuss the origin of nature. At that time, scientific thinking was becoming quite stylish, many people entertaining the possibility that the Earth was not a flat surface with a canopy of sky and stars above, as well as other outlandish ideas, such as natural laws rather than emotional deities ruled the planet.

So it was that these three great thinkers held a summit meeting on top of the highest mountain. They meditated for some time before the Wizard spoke, saying he was very concerned about the popularity of the new science and that a little fake knowledge was a dangerous thing. Also, he added, science is rather bad for the business of wizardry. I concur, joined in the Witch. I am considering casting a nasty spell on all these vile scientistas, perhaps turning them into monkeys, showing the world what buffoons they are. The Shaman held his tongue.

The Summit continued for days, the Wizard and the Witch evolving their strategy to curb the belief in science. When they were done, they asked the Shaman to spin a tale refuting all the scientific hullabaloo and preserving the truth about the nature of the universe. And so, the Shaman rolled up his sleeves, smiled and said this. To my mind, it's all quite simple. In the beginning there was a whole lot of nothing. Then God Almighty, the Greatest of All Magicians, clapped his hands, and, presto pronto, a Big Bang exploded, from which a Universe was born on top of our perfectly flat planet adorned by a canopy of stars. He chuckled, adding, That should put science to rest forever.

# The Woman Who Prepared

Once there was a woman who prepared. She lived with two friends downtown. Instead of waiting around for the perfect man to appear at her front door, she decided to take matters into her own hands and act as though that Mr. Right was already in her life. So, this is what she did. She took herself out to dinner and imagined her man sitting across from her, smiling and eyes glued to her.

She also went to the Saturday night movies with him, walked on the beach with him, and they hiked in the woods and up by Bear Mountain together. She sent herself a box of her favorite dark chocolates with a gift card that read, Love from Yours Truly. And when her birthday came, she received her favorite Gucci Envy perfume from guess who.

Her two room-mates thought she was loony and searched for men on the social networks and in neighborhood pubs, but the woman who prepared ignored their ridicule and continued to pursue her own line of reasoning which went like this. If you want something, you gotta give it to yourself first.

So, it came to be that one day she went to the local church and, when nobody was looking, she married herself. She wrote up some vows, recited them perfectly and put a ring on her own finger. When she went home, she popped open a bottle of champagne, and sat down opposite her imaginary partner. At that very moment, the doorbell rang so she went to open the door.

Standing right there was the man of her dreams, holding a beautiful bouquet of red roses. Delivery man, he said, and smiled. So, she let him in.

# The Empty Woman

A woman felt empty at her core. In fact, her life was full, but deep down inside she felt a supreme sense of emptiness. She had tried to run away from it, filling herself up, but now there was no getting away. She was an empty woman.

So, she said good-bye to her family and embarked on a pilgrimage across the planet. She climbed the highest mountain and breathed all her breaths until she felt breathless. Still, she felt empty. So, she returned home, but her house was empty, her feeling of emptiness now overflowing. She went to an old wishing well to see if she could refill herself. Pulling up the bucket, she came up with a wise old owl, who winked at her and offered this advice. You're not going to fill up your emptiness with this sort of well. Go to the Source of all Emptiness and ask to be replenished there.

So, while trying to understand his words, she could not imagine where the Source of All Emptiness might be located. Thus, she found herself sitting at an oasis in the middle of a desert, empty as the night sky above. She knew not how she got there and just sat there empty- headed. As she was about to give up all hope, a shooting star came down and sat beside her. He held out a glass of glittering liquid and said, Welcome to Ground Zero. From this point all fullness comes. Here, drink this. And so, she drank the glass of all that glitters, fell asleep and dreamed of grasshoppers.

When she awoke the next morning, a frog sat next to her, smiled, and said, well, let's get hopping. So, they went galloping off together across the desert on a seahorse.

Bob Mandel

# The Man Who Lost His Head

◇◇◇◇◇◇◇◇◇◇◇◇◇◇◇◇◇◇◇◇

There existed a man who thought he lost his head. Maybe he did and maybe he didn't. He woke up one morning, looked in a mirror and saw himself headless. At first, he thought it was impossible since he was looking in the mirror so he must have eyes and therefore a head, but when he reached for his head it was empty space.

The more he thought, the more he thought he really had lost his head, but had the sensation of the lost head, like people who lose an arm can still feel it. When he went out and walked down the street, however, his neighbors didn't look at him strangely, as if he were a man with no head, but smiled at him in a very normal way. Arriving at his office, his secretary winked and handed him his messages as always. So, he went into his office, sat down, and began thinking, soon arriving at the thought that maybe it wasn't his head that he lost but his mind, whereupon he made an appointment with a friend, a psychiatrist, and went to see him.

His friend greeted him warmly and offered a drink, but the man shook his, well, shook the memory of his head. The two men entered the psychiatrist's office and the doctor asked what was up. I've lost my head, he replied. I mean, do you see my head? His friend examined him for a moment, for the first time giving him a good looking over, and then replied, Of course I see your head. What's going on? The man felt a tear bubbling in his eye and then he noticed a reflection of himself in a window.

What he saw looking back at him was his head, good as ever, but hanging there alone, the entire rest of his body nowhere to be seen.

# The Very Gifted Woman

In ancient days there lived a very gifted woman who could see the future. Trouble was, nobody wanted to hear what she had to say. She walked around shouting her visions, such as, some day there will be trains, do you know about airplanes, how about those new iPhones, and what about those robotics? Nobody could care less and, in fact, people would cross the street when they saw her coming, no doubt with some new cock and bull story about social networks and satellites in outer space, whatever that was.

Years passed and the very gifted woman grew tired of nobody listening, so she came up with a new plan for channeling her special gift. She got a big crystal ball and set up a stall at the market place where she sold her wares under the guise of "Madam Futura Knows Yours". Suddenly, long lines formed. She would look into her globe and tell one woman about her husband's betrayal, another man about his financial ruin, and still others about coming challenges with pregnancy, birth, and bad kids. Her prophecies were so accurate she amassed quite a fortune for her readings.

Then, there came a day when a man entered her tent, sat down, and folded his arms. What do you want, Madam Futura asked? Well, he said, you tell me. I mean, considering you are the one who seduced me, thus the ruin of my marriage, embezzled my financial empire, thus my ruin, and corrupted my children, thus their ruin, I suggest you cease this business at once or I will expose you as a charlatan, or perhaps an extortioner.

So, it was the very gifted woman closed shop and moved to a nearby kingdom where she set up a new stall for Past Life Readings, shopping her gifts in a most flattering and inoffensive manner.

Bob Mandel

# The Dirty Boy

There came a time when God appeared as a dirty little boy standing outside a church. You cannot enter, said the priest, so God walked off. The reason He was dirty was because he had been playing with the animals down by the river. He went back down there and they all rolled over him, so happy to be with Him and breathe His lovely scent. Then God went swimming down the river and when He emerged He noticed another church, but the priest said He could not enter because He was naked.

So, God went away. He climbed up a mountain, the highest mountain in all the world, and exclaimed, I am God Almighty, the mightiest of all rulers and the King of the Universe, and the people of this planet blasphemy me by forbidding me entrance to their places of worship. I hereby declare that from this day hence, the only true temple shall be the cathedral of Nature-- the canopies of the forests, mountains, valleys, rivers, and plains. If anyone seeks me, he shall find me there. Nobody heard Him and things continued as always.

Several millennia later the churches lay empty in ruin and people could not find their God anywhere. One day a dirty little boy appeared down by the river and everyone remembered.

# The Married Couple

◇◇◇◇◇◇◇◇◇◇◇◇◇◇◇

A man and a woman sit opposite each other, he drinking his morning coffee, she sipping her herbal tea. They do not speak. In truth, they reside in a gorgeous townhouse in one of the most fashionable neighborhoods in town. However, they do not look at each other. The lovely house is stone cold quiet. He rises and goes to his office.

He is a professor of psychology at Brooklyn College, and thus he goes to read some papers. Then he heads for the library where he looks for some books about relationships, trying to understand what is happening. She washes the dishes from last night's dinner, takes a long bath, then meditates to calm her frazzled nerves.

Later, she is working in her garden when a stranger appears. He identifies himself as a messenger, hands her an envelope, then disappears. She puts the envelope in her pocket, continues gardening, and begins humming.

Meanwhile, the man, finding nothing of interest in the library, goes off to teach his classes for the day, one about dreams and the other about desires. When he returns home, the woman remains out in the garden, back to him. So, he pours himself a tumbler of 18 year old Scotch whiskey and sits on the porch, watching her in silence.

Feeling his eyes tickle her back, she turns, smiles genuinely, gathers her tools, and, coming up to the porch, sets them down and sits next to him. How was your day? She asks. He looks as her, as if surprised by her question. We received a message today, she tells him. A message? He is curious. Yes, she continues, a messenger came and handed me this note. She takes the message out of the pocket of her well-worn gardening apron, and hands it to him. He reads it. He smiles. She smiles. He repeats the words out loud. Every dream is a desire. Every desire is a dream. The greatest desire of all is the dream of love.

Bob Mandel

# The Second Son of God

God is pacing at the pearly gate waiting for an important message. He has sent his most trusted advisor down to Earth to offer the leaders of all the countries a very special and extraordinary deal. His Angel Michael is three days late and our good Lord is a bit concerned. Thus, God is pacing.

Meanwhile, down on Earth Michael is in the midst of heated negotiations with the leaders of the world. This is the offer God asked him to present to them.

If the leaders are willing to join together in a massive effort to clean up the planet, end all wars, dismantle all their weapons of mass destruction, recall all assault weapons, put an end to all crimes against humanity, and erase all hunger, disease, poverty, and ignorance—if they accomplish all these mighty tasks, then as a reward and a great blessing God will send a new and wonderful Messiah, a second Prince of Peace, his second born son after Jesus.

The leaders have been going back and forth over the fine points of the deal, but finally they all agree. Michael returns to God and reports the good news. God stops pacing. The leaders keep their part of the deal. Then God sends his second born son to Earth, the new Prince of Peace.

The child wakes up in the maternity ward of a very fine hospital, an angelic midwife and a smiling doula by his side. He is surrounded by all the world leaders. He takes a breath and says to the gathering. So, I hear you all cleaned up your act. They all shake their heads and murmur yes. Well done, says the child. Now I want to go home because I miss my daddy very much.

# The Banjo Man

There once was a man who thought he was God. He lived near the Botanical Gardens and learned his craft preaching to the flowers, all of whom perked up when he started talking to them. Later, he went around telling all the people up and down the borough that God spoke through him, and if they listened all would be well. He walked down every street in town, standing on a soapbox and announcing to people that he and they were all the voices of God. But nobody listened, thinking he was a harmless lunatic.

Then one day, back in the gardens he started playing a banjo and the flowers started dancing. The kids began to think he was cool. So, when he told them to follow him out to the lake, they followed him like he was some kind of Pied Piper, only a banjo type.

So, every day he played the banjo and talked about God, and shined his light from his twinkly eyes. Word got around about this Banjo Man and before too long kids and their parents were hanging out by the lake to hear what the man who thought he was God would say.

One day, he stopped playing in the middle of a tune and said. My friends, I am a man and I am God and I believe we are all human and we are God too. The problem is this. Instead of behaving as the beautiful God- people you are, you spend most of your days behaving like a bunch of jackasses, which you aint, and that is why this sweet world has turned so sour.

So, good people, now I will play the banjo again, which he did, and soon most everyone forgot what he had said.

Except for the children.

# The Woman Who Lost Time

Once there was a woman who lost time. She literally didn't know what day it was. She walked through a sort of eternal twilight, not knowing her birthday from Valentine's Day, Christmas from Easter Sunday. Needless to say, Mother's Day was unknown to her, as were the days of all the saints.

One day, the woman found herself walking across the Golden Gate Bridge in San Francisco. It was a typical, foggy day and the woman got lost on her way, all turned around, so while she believed she was headed one way she was, in fact, going back where she came from.

Suddenly, she stopped and looked over the side of the bridge where the fog lifted like a veil, a light began to glow, and she could see down into the San Francisco Bay. A school of bottle nose dolphins appeared, dancing and playing joyfully. The woman took a deep breath and yearned for that feeling, drawn to the dolphins below. Just at that moment, a gentleman in an overcoat, bowler hat, and an umbrella raised over his head, approached the woman. As it was not raining, the woman became curious. The man said to her. Do you have the time? The woman, flabbergasted, looked at her watch but could not make heads or tails of all the numbers. I'm afraid I lost my time, she replied, whereupon the gentleman took her by the arm, raised his umbrella, and they both leaped off the Golden Gate Bridge.

Instead of falling into the bay, however, they lifted up into the sky, the umbrella carrying them high above the fog bank and the clouds to a distant star, where they landed at a castle in the sand. Inside the castle they discovered a short man, maybe an elf, in a huge room with many clocks and timepieces all over the place. The man introduced himself as Father Time and proceeded to show them how he spun time from a magical spinning wheel. The gentleman smiled at such a marvel. The woman clapped her hands in joy and asked Father Time. Dear Father, could you perhaps find for me the time I have lost? The Father scratched his long beard, then twitched his bushy eyebrow, whereupon he announced. I'm afraid that time lost is irretrievable, young lady, but I'd be happy, delighted even, to spin you a bundle of fresh woven time, guaranteed to last a lifetime, which is just what he did before sending the happy woman and the kind gentleman off to live happily ever after, or not.

# A Certain Antelope

◇◇◇◇◇◇◇◇◇◇◇◇◇◇◇◇

A boy is walking to meet a friend in the Heights when he is interrupted by a certain antelope who asks for directions. Normally, antelope do not visit this area, but this particular year a few antelope certainly appeared, unannounced. The boy, startled, offers to help and suggest the antelope go a certain way, then continues to his meeting with his friend. When he joins up with his friend, the friend tells him about a certain antelope he also met on the way and they realize there is a certain coincidence, something serendipity going on.

So, they go looking for a certain antelope, assuming they encountered the same one, as it is very unusual to encounter an antelope in Brooklyn. They go down to the river and ask a fisherman if he's seen a certain antelope, which he has not, and so they go out to Marine Fields where there is much wilderness, but no one has spotted an antelope. Feeling defeated, the two boys head back downtown where they spot two antelope walking out of a local watering hole. Locking eyes with each other, the boys then run over to the two antelope and try to discern which one is the certain antelope.

So, they ask the antelope, did either of you meet up with either of us this morning? The two antelope look at each other, then shake their heads. Not me, says one. Nor me, echoes the other. Are you certain, the boys ask in unison? Absolutely certain, the two antelope respond. Thus, it was that two boys found two certain antelope.

# The Kind King

⬦⬦⬦⬦⬦⬦⬦⬦⬦⬦⬦

A long time ago there lived a very wise old King who was also very kind. This was in the early days, before politics divided folks. Loving people came from all over the land to seek his advice and guidance on all sorts of matters ranging from finances to romances. Although he was not strong, the King freely offered his suggestions, never refusing a request nor asking for anything in return.

The King grew older and his health was failing. As he was very beloved, people wanted to help him but he refused all offers, saying the best medicine was continuing comforting others.

One day a young boy, tears trickling down his face, came to the King. He explained that his father was very ill, too sick to travel, so please, would the King pay him a visit. The King said he was neither a doctor nor well enough to travel. However, when the boy told him all the doctors in the land had tried to heal his father but could not, he agreed to visit the man.

So, they journeyed across the flatlands to a certain house where the boy and his father lived alone. When they arrived, the King observed the father working in his garden. Unsteady on his feet, he hobbled towards the man as the boy stood back. A conversation transpired after which the father kissed the King who then told the boy, all was well. When the King departed, the father said to the son. Well done, my boy, and they both went off to take care of the sheep.

The next morning, the King awakened, and feeling mysteriously rejuvenated, resumed his acts of loving kindness.

# God's New Creation

A new world was coming. Everyone could feel it, waiting to be born. But what would happen to the old world? Nobody knew. So it was that the people gathered on the street in front of the House of God, hoping for clarification.

Meanwhile, inside the house, an uneasy calm prevailed. God was busy, at work inside His Globe Room, completing His magnificent spherical mural. On the floor beneath Him He had painted the people, their faces looking up towards Heaven, many colors, ages, and expressions, some confused, others curious. On the round walls climbing up towards the dome ceiling stretched long arms, hands beseeching, fingers pointing, praying, some clenched in fists of overcoming. And up above, the Light appeared, the Light of Heaven, glowing, emanating, and radiating, pure and palpable, and flowing down from the dome, showering the room with an ethereal iridescence, lighting God Himself standing on a ladder in the middle.

God observed his masterpiece, but felt something was missing, yet He could not say what. Outside, the people grew restless as darkness descended, and began to turn to go back to their previous life, thinking it was not yet time for a new world. Just then, the door opened, and God Himself appeared, bathed in immense Light spilling out from inside. Come in, my children, He invited them. Come into My home and complete my Creation. Be the Light with Me.

# The Rainbow Dome

Back in the day, the flatlands of the long island were among the best in the area, the soil moist and rich so things grew better than closer to the city. One day a farm boy looked up and exclaimed, Oh my God. Will ya look at that? As he was talking to himself, he received no reply. Far away, over on the north shore, another fertile place for agriculture, a girl tending to chickens, also saw it. Holy cow, she cried out. I don't believe my own two eyes. Meanwhile, a window washer, hanging from the eleventh floor of a newly constructed high-rise building downtown, went spinning on his cable in disbelief.

So it was, throughout the island and neighboring lands, people shouted out in wonder and awe, as if the sky itself were falling. And what was it that knocked their socks off? Just this! The entire sky had turned into a dome of rainbows with the sun at the pinnacle and rays of colors streaming down as far as the eye could see.

Oh, my God, people declared. Holy Moses! Of course, they all wondered what it could mean.

Religious leaders debated the message from above. Scientists researched changes in the atmosphere and influences from outer space. Politicians argued various conspiracy theories. Finally, after much discussion back and forth, it was decided that nobody knew the cause, but no harm done. It was a beautiful thing, so let it be.

Time passed. One day it began to rain. It rained and rained and rained. For days and weeks and months. And thus, all the colors of all the dome of rainbows came pouring down, painting all the land and sea, all the farms and forests, barns and buildings, birds and animals, a stunning array of magical colors. In the end, not even the people were spared from the beauty.

Bob Mandel

# The Boy Who Died Too Young

Once there was a boy who died too young. It was tragic, really. He was climbing a ladder to retrieve a frisbee from the roof for his little sister standing below when a huge gust of wind came out of nowhere and knocked the young lad to his premature fall.

When the boy got to heaven, he complained. That just wasn't fair, Mr. God, he said. I was just at the very beginning of my life and I had high hopes for my future. Plus, I left my parents on the farm in the lurch and also my sister who worshiped the ground I walked on. God, moved by the young boy's complaint, sent him back for a second go-round at life.

So it was that the boy woke up under the ladder with a bad headache, but no worse for wear. He grew up, but, if truth be told, his life was very hard. The day after he fell off the ladder, his parents were both killed in a tractor accident. He and his sister were raised in an orphanage. Then he had problems with drugs and alcohol. He ended up in prison for a crime he did not commit and he died there at a very old age.

When he arrived back in heaven God said to him. Good to see you again, my boy. How did it go for you? The boy who died too young but now was quite old looked at God, totally bewildered. Do I know you, he asked? Have we met before? So, God told him the story of his first visit to Heaven, hoping to jog the man's memory. The old man, remembering, said to God. I thought it was a dream. I can't believe it was true. What were you thinking, Mr. God? You're supposed to be the Almighty Lord. You surely could see what would become of me if you sent me back. What in your name were you thinking? God looked at the man and nodded with understanding. Well, son, I can see how you would feel how you feel, but I was only thinking you didn't want to be in Heaven so I thought I'd show you how the other folk lived.

# The Shadow Boxer

In the old days, down at Gleason's gym, there was a famous shadow boxer. He never actually fought against another person as he was a peaceful man who would never harm a fly. Still, he loved the craft of fisticuffs and busied himself going against some of the best shadows in the borough. After training at Gleason's, the shadow boxer moved out onto the streets. You could see him dancing down Fulton St., punching away at imaginary opponents, people moving out of his way as he cut quite a wide swath, dodging windmills and japing at thin air.

Then it came to pass one dark night as the feller was boxing his way along Eastern Parkway up by the Grand Army Plaza that the shadow boxer took an uppercut from some unknown shadow and they found him the next morning lying there covered in blood. He wasn't dead or nothing, but he was mumbling all sorts of nonsense about some white ghost that had jumped out of an alley and sucker-punched him. According to the shadow boxer, he got back up on his feet and matched that ghost blow for blow.

Well, after that incident, the shadow boxer wasn't quite the same. He continued his fancy footwork and his arms still stabbed at windmills, as it were, but he was somewhat tilted, as if he could not see straight. Thus, his magnificence suffered a severe blow. Nonetheless, he continued to command the respect of the community, people recognizing his situation while respecting who he once was. Eventually, he slipped away, as though disappearing into the night, never heard from again and nobody knowing what had become of the sweet feller.

Yet, it is said until this day if you walk around Eastern Parkway, out by the Grand Army Plaza, on certain dark nights you can hear the swishing of the boxing gloves as the shadow boxer and the white ghost continue to battle it out to determine the true champion of the world.

Bob Mandel

# The Clamor of Angels

All of God's angels were clamoring for his attention. Michael tearfully told of the devastation to Mother Nature, the climate change, pollution, and terrible wildfire ravaging the Earth. Gabriel passionately explained how communication among the people was disrespectful and hateful, how the media was rampant with fake news, and how the written word could no longer be believed. Raphael pleaded with God to do something to save the poor children who were dying unnecessarily from famine, disease, and poor drinking water.

In short, God was beseeched by his most beloved angels to rescue his children in dire need down below. God took in all the feedback, thanked his angels, then withdrew to his study to meditate.

Three days later, he returned to address his devoted and beloved angels. I have decided, dear angels. I will send signs to the people, extreme warnings to them with devastating storms, plagues, earthquakes, melting icecaps and gigantic tidal waves burying their coastlines and cities. Maybe then they will heed my words and correct their ways.

A massive hush fell upon all the angels that lasted for a timeless moment, whereupon Gabriel, the spokesman for the group, said this. Dear Father, all these things you threaten to wreak upon the people, you have already done so. That is what we're clamoring about.

# The Knight of Loving Kindness

A boy runs out of his house without even wishing his mom a good day. He is in a rush to meet his friends and see what trouble they can make. The boy has forgotten right from wrong and just wants to feel like he belongs to the group.

Suddenly, he sees a man in black coming at him.

He makes a quick decision, darts across the street and runs away. His heart is beating fast as he slows down and turns the corner, only to see the same man in black walking straight towards him. About-facing, the boy runs back around the block a second time and, thinking he has escaped, walks into the park and sits down on a bench. Hello, says the man in black, sitting down next to him.

Oh, my God, says the boy. Don't be afraid of me. I am afraid of you. Very afraid. Do you know who I am? You're the man in black from the Temple of the Dome. And you are a smart young man! Boy, the boy says. I'm only a boy. Come with me, the man in black suggests, and the boy follows him to the Temple of the Dome. They enter, climb down a huge stairway that goes into an ancient crypt where there is a labyrinth. It is dark, but there is a glowing light so the way is illuminated. They walk into the labyrinth which coils to a center-point where they stand, surrounded by tall stones that maybe are swords, or sunflowers.

What comes next, asks the boy, his fear slowly replaced by a sense of adventure? Now, says the man in black, lifting one of the swords out of the ground, now I anoint you as the Knight of Loving Kindness. And he dubs the boy three times on the top of his head.

Every morning, when you awaken, you will receive your mission for the day, your special assignment. You must do it. How will I know? The boy asks. You will know.

The next morning, the boy wakes up and knows nothing. No mission. No Knight. No man in black. He runs out of the house again without even wishing his mom a good day. He goes to school, disappointed. His teacher greets him with a friendly smile, which is strange, because the day before he had reprimanded him for being unkind to a fellow student he had called a bad word. The teacher, his smile seeming genuine, asks him. Did you complete your homework assignment? The boy, confused, looks up at him, shrugs his shoulders, and says maybe he forgot.

Later, the boy is in study hall, trying to remember his homework assignment and whether it is the same as his special assignment as a Knight of Loving Kindness. Suddenly, he remembers. Everything comes back to him. He races home where his mother greets him at the door. What is it, my son? What's the matter? The boy, teary- eyed, replies. Nothing, mom. I just forgot to wish you a good day this morning. In fact, I forgot a lot of mornings.

I am so sorry. And, so it was the boy completed his first assignment as a Knight of Loving Kindness.

# The Wonderful Witch
## of Balderdash

~~~~~~~~~~~~~~~~~~

She lived down by the park and took off from her rooftop every night. She wasn't a wicked witch, not a mean bone in her body. She was just keeping an eye out for a certain missing person, but we'll get back to him later.

On a clear night, you could see her on her ratty old broom, sailing across the moon and stars, tipping her hat and waving kindly. A blessing. Neighbors did testify, however, that she would swoop down without any notice and peep through the curtains to observe what was going on in their inner sanctums. It could be quite nerve-wracking really. There you'd be, brushing your teeth before turning in for the night and, Holy Moses, that darn witch of Balderdash would be smiling at you through the bathroom window, clearly needing a good brushing of her own.

So, it went on, but no one reported her because if truth be told, she was a very kind witch, leaving candy for the children, reading books to the elderly, and whispering sweet words of wisdom into exhausted mothers' ears as they fell asleep. Nevertheless, a witch being a witch, she was of some danger to her very handsome husband. You see, although he adored her to death and would never look twice at another woman, the kind witch of Balderdash got it into her head that he was sneaking around. It was a whole lot of nonsense, no doubt, but the witch from Balderdash couldn't tell nonsense from good sense.

Thus it was, she flew all over the neighborhood like a crazy banshee in pursuit of her prey, while all the while her handsome husband slept alone in their bed, dreaming of his magical wife, unaware of her absence.

One morning, as the Kind Witch of Balderdash returned from her nocturnal rounds, she entered the bedroom and, not finding her handsome husband present, entered a state of altered reality. Discovering him brushing his teeth in the bathroom, her eyes popped out of her

Bob Mandel

head and she exclaimed Aha! Whereupon, she chased him in his boxers out the front door, down the stairs, and out onto the boulevard, where she pursued him, twirling the broom over her head, screeching and hollering as the poor man darted in and out of alleys while the entire neighborhood looked out their windows, cheering on the lovebirds.

# The Three Questions

〰〰〰〰〰〰〰〰〰

It was graduation time at the University of Heaven. God was interviewing all the students for their assignments in the new world he was creating. He asked each person the same three questions. What could you do best? How could you make the biggest difference? What would make you most happy? When the three answers were identical, the student graduated and received God's blessing and proceeded to the new world. When the answers were different, they returned to the university for an extra year of study.

So it was that God came to interview the last student, a young woman with a blank look on her face. What could you do best, He asked? Whatever you want, she replied. God sat up straight. How could you make the biggest difference, He asked? However you want, she answered. God smiled. What would make you most happy, God finally asked her? Whatever would make you most happy, she smiled. God took a breath and said to the young lady. Maybe you misunderstand my questions. I want to know what you want, not what I want. She nodded her head, paused, and then replied.

I understand, sir, but what I most want to know is what you want.

Bob Mandel

# The Saint of Kings County

One day a saint arrived. They called her The Saint of Kings County, but she brushed aside all such anointments, having no desire for sainthood. Here is what happened, how she came to be known as so special.

Rosie was a teenage girl who had to drop out of school due to her family's circumstances, being the eldest of five children, the only girl and money scarce. Being a qualified nurse at the time, she landed a position at Kings County Hospital, assisting at the maternity ward. These were the days during the war when the babies were booming in Brooklyn as much as the bombs were dropping over there in Europe. There was a shortage of nurse midwives and Rosie had a knack with the midwifery thing, thereby finding herself delivering many a fine baby into the world.

One day in particular, August 6, 1945, the very same day they dropped the big bomb on Hiroshima, ten babies burst into this world at Kings County in the space of a couple of hours. Rosie was said to have delivered each and every one, a whirling dervish of midwifery -- some easy, others complicated, one with forceps and another all backwards, but all of them made it to their new lives with no damage done. In fact, they said that each and every one of those newbies came into the world with a special kind of light flying out of their eyes, and a smile you couldn't resist.

Word got around that it was Rosie's kind and loving hands blessed their arrival with a bit of divine sparkle. So came her reputation as an angel of the neighborhood and a saint to all newborns. As for Rosie, she returned home, sat on her bed, and cried for relief and joy all the night long. The next morning, she handed her dad the money for a month's rent and went back to the hospital for another shift. Her dad watched her walk off, her hands stuffed into her woolen coat. A real saint, he thought.

# The Swimming Lesson

A boy wanted to learn to swim so he asked his dad to teach him. The dad scratched his beard, thought about it, and agreed. The next morning, bright and early, father and son went out to a lake, where they sat down by the edge. The father instructed the boy just to look at the lake for a while.

While they sat in silence, the father remembered how his own father taught him to swim. They were up in the Adirondacks when one day his dad declared, today's the day you learn to swim. So, he took him out to the river and threw him in, shouting, SWIM, SWIM, MY BOY. The boy sank down, rose up, splashing and gasping for air, praying not to drown and make it back to shore. Pretty good, his dad had said. Let's try again. And again. Until the son was swimming like a fish.

When do I learn to swim, his own son now asked him many years later? You are learning, the father replied. This is the first step. Tell me, when you look at the water, when you think about it, how do you feel? I feel like I want to get in and swim, dad. Of course, you do. And you will. But first tell me, do you feel like the water is your friend or something to be conquered? Without hesitation, the boy said. Something to be conquered. Maybe, said his dad. But if you see the water as a friend, then you can play with it, swim with it, and enjoy it without fear. The boy considered such an idea, but then shook his head, rejecting it. No, dad. I think I need to conquer it. Whereupon the father, understanding, took the boy out to the deep end of the lake, lifted him high in the air, and threw him in the lake. SWIM, he shouted. SWIM, MY BOY. When the boy emerged from the water, he was smiling, happy as a clam. Dad! Dad, he cried out.

I just made friends with the water.

# The Glitter and the Glow

✕✕✕✕✕✕✕✕✕✕✕✕✕✕✕✕✕

A man is driving his old beat-up pickup truck down the highway, his heart heavy and his mind troubled. You see, his wife's got a breast cancer, his son is in the military overseas, and his daughter is pregnant and married to an abusive drunkard. When the man sees a young lady hitchhiking by the side of the road, he pulls over to give her a lift. They drive off and he notices she is a sparkling young lady, full of glitter and glow. For some reason, he starts talking and pours his heart out to her while she just sits there, glittering and glowing. When he is finished with his story, she says, don't worry, everything will work out, and he looks over but she is no longer there. She has vanished into thin air. Some months later, things are looking up for the man. His wife has had a remission and is back to full health again. His son is home from overseas and enrolled in the university. And his daughter has divorced the bum who was mistreating her and has a beautiful baby girl.

One day the man is driving his old beat-up pickup truck down the road again, the truck huffing and puffing to get where it's going, and he sees the same hitchhiker again. She hops in, glittering and glowing as before, so he tells her all his good news. She smiles, and he asks how he can repay her for her blessing. She tells him, so he drives her to the next town where she goes to an ATM, returns to his driver's window, hands him $2000, and says, get your truck fixed.

# The Bicycle

A boy is riding his bike on the old railroad track at the far end of the island. He meets his grandfather at an abandoned train station. His grandfather has a surprise for him in the back of his beat-up pickup truck, a shiny new red bicycle. Telling him to take good care of it, the old man drives off.

The boy mounts his new bike and follows the railroad tracks which haven't been used in many a year. The rusty old rails climb up and the boy grows tired, so he stops to soak his feet in a stream. He sees an old Indian man walking towards him. He says to the boy, If you ride your shiny new bike around that lake over there, you will come to a cave, maybe a tunnel. He points ahead. If you enter and go to the innermost chamber, you will meet someone who wants to talk to you.

So, the boy rides his bike around the lake, finds what looks like an old railroad tunnel, dismounts his bike, and enters the darkness, moving slowly, going to the deepest part. He hears someone breathing and calls out, Hello. Hello? Hello, comes an echo. And then he sees a boy, an Indian boy sitting on a rock. The boy approaches. Do you want to talk to me? Yes. My grandfather said you would come and give me a new bicycle. The boy with the bike says, but why would I do that? Because your people took away our land and you giving me the bike is a sign of love.

The boy with the bike thinks about this for some time and then says OK, and gives him the bike. The two boys stand face to face for some time, each considering his next step. Finally, the boy says. My bike is your bike. The Indian boy nods and replies. Thank you. You are my brother.

# The Heart of Gold

◇◇◇◇◇◇◇◇◇◇◇◇◇◇

A gold miner is chipping away, searching for a heart of gold, when he feels a tapping on his shoulder, looks up, and finds himself staring at a pixie. She shakes her head. Not there, she says, follow me, and slips out of the cave. The gold miner, not believing he has seen a pixie, continues chipping. Then the tapping returns on his shoulder, this time the pixie tugging on his shirt as well, and she says, Seriously, I know where the gold is. Come on.

So he goes with her down the river to a labyrinth of stones. She tells him he is too large to enter and she must diminish him. While he does not like the idea, he imagines the gold, so he nods, she snaps her fingers and reduces him to her size. They enter the labyrinth, dark and cold, he follows her.

When they arrive at the center, a Fairy Queen sits on a throne of stone and asks what they seek. The pixie replies, my friend desires a heart of gold. A worthy goal, declares the Fairy Queen, providing he has a worthy heart. I do, exclaims the man, I truly do. She looks deeply into his soul and sighs. Men, she says, how can you believe what they say? At that moment, the little pixie suffers a terrible convulsion, rolls over and, tears dripping down her cheeks, tells the digger she is dying and he must get out of the labyrinth fast or else he too will die. Gazing at his beloved friend and guide, he tells her he cannot abandon her, whereupon the Fairy Queen declares, my dear gold miner, you have found your heart of gold. The pixie then opens her eyes, winks, and tells the digger, I also know where the other gold is.

# A Very Little Pebble

A boy holds a very little pebble in his hand. He gazes at it with all his might. Aha, he says to himself. He shows it to his best friend, who says simply, it's just a pebble. He brings it home to show his sister, who laughs. At dinner, he introduces his pebble to his parents, telling them he found a new friend. Very good, they say, as they eat their fish and chips. The next morning, the boy brings his pebble to school, and reveals it to his class. This is my new friend, and he is magical. His classmates laugh, and his teacher talks about geology. Very good, he tells the boy.

Aha, the boy thinks. At lunchtime, he heads off to the hills, climbing up a very big mountain, far too tall for a little boy to climb. On the way, he meets a squirrel and shows him the pebble. The squirrel smiles and points up the mountain, following the boy as he heads up. Farther on, the boy encounters a wolf, who, examining the pebble, motions for the boy to follow him. They continue to climb. Near the top, they meet a shaman, a shape-shifter, who is half man, half goat. The shape- shifter asks for the pebble, and the boy reluctantly hands it over.

Soon, they arrive at the pinnacle—the boy, squirrel, wolf, and shape-shifter. The shaman rubs the pebble between his hands, then gives it to the wolf who rolls it in his mouth before giving it to the squirrel, who places it on the ground for the little boy.

Aha, the boy says as he rolls the little pebble down the gigantic mountain, where it gains momentum and emits a golden steam, gathering, collecting, and accumulating a luminescent energy, snowballing into a gigantic golden globe, a great ball of fire, larger than the moon, sparkling gold, rolling, descending, and depositing itself into the largest sea in the universe with a fabulous, cataclysmic roar and upheaval. Hallelujah! A new planet is born from a very little pebble.

Bob Mandel

# The Return of Moses

◇◇◇◇◇◇◇◇◇◇◇◇◇◇◇

There came a day when Moses went back up the mountain to talk to God, who greeted him enthusiastically. Moses, Moses, my prodigal son, Moses. Where have you been all this time? Busy, busy, my Father. Always some dispute to settle or child to comfort. You know how it is. God shook his head all-knowingly.

So, what can I do for you this time, Moses? Is everything OK with the commandments? Well, yes, and no. That's what I came to talk to you about. Oy. You mean the people want to renegotiate? Again? Not exactly, Father, and I mean no disrespect, but there's something not quite right about the whole deal. Hmm, God replied, and mumbled under his breath. Sit down, Moses, and tell me the problem.

So it was that God and Moses sat opposite each other and had it out, a good face-to-face. You see, my Father, the whole idea of commanding that your children obey you, you and you only, and that they be grateful to you always, smacks of a constant need for attention, a kind of narcissism, if you know what I mean. God took a deep breath, trying to understand Moses' point. You mean, the people think the commandments are about me and not lessons for them to learn? It could be, replied Moses, who mumbled something under his breath. Hmm, said God. Do you have a suggestion, Moses? A solution, perhaps? Just so, Father. My idea is this. Instead of commanding such respect from your children, you could give them one precious gift which would allow them to discover love and gratitude by themselves, without obligation. Oh? God lifted an eyebrow in genuine curiosity.

And what is this precious gift you refer to? Freedom, Moses replied. You could give them the freedom to discover the truth for themselves. Hmm. God smiled, considering the offer. You mean, let my people go? Exactly! And so, God and Moses went back and forth, sparks flying, for some time until finally God said. Moses, what you propose is admirable, desirable, and very wise. There is only one glitch. A glitch? Asked Moses.

Yes, a glitch. You see, Moses, the people already possess this freedom you mention. I put it in their souls from Day One. Oh, replied Moses. I didn't know. Then he went down the mountain, mumbling under his breath.

# The Coast is Clear

✕✕✕✕✕✕✕✕✕✕✕✕

The Anomalies on the bridge settled down. They lived in teepees, fished in the river below, and created sustainable raised bed gardens for food. The group that had returned to forage in the old world had not been heard from, nor had the futurists who ventured into the unknown.

On the bridge, there were days of gorgeous light, days of fog, and days of complete darkness, which the people came to recognize as the three states of their minds. Their leader who was called Solomon preached patience and kindness, and for the most part the people were good. There were factions, however, one which advocated returning to the past to meet their brothers who ventured there and another who pushed for packing up and heading forwards where the futurists had disappeared a long time ago. Solomon reminded them that when they first divided into three tribes, they had agreed to stay on the bridge, a midway point. And so they had settled down, and all things considered, thrived.

One day a whistle sounded, announcing the arrival of strangers. Only they were not strangers, they were the tribe who had returned to the past. They were ragged and worn, thirsty and hungry. Once they were revived, they explained that the past had closed in on them, and they could no longer forage to survive. Finally, they made their way to the bridge again, just as the Old World was disappearing behind them. It literally went up in smoke. And so it was that two of the three tribes were reunited on the bridge, enriched by their diversity and integration.

But as the years passed, the conditions on the bridge deteriorated. Sustainable farming was suffering from a prolonged drought. The fish in the river became sick and insufficient. What was worst of all, the people were losing all hope, their patience and kindness growing thin. Soon, their stress, tension, and frustration escalated near to violence. Just when everyone seemed to have forgotten about the Futurists, Solomon rang a bell one foggy day and, lo and behold, a glow appeared in the distance and they arrived, beings of light from the far side of the bridge, waving their hands with smiles on their faces and greetings of love and laughter in the air. Bringing fresh food, flowers, gifts from the future-- children flying kites of dragons, unicorns, and piggies. Aloha! Aloha, they called to their long-lost brothers and sisters. Come. Come. Follow us. The coast is clear.

Printed in the United States
by Baker & Taylor Publisher Services